COUGAR HALLOWEEN MISCHIEF

A NOVELLA

TERRY SPEAR

Cougar Halloween Mischief

Copyright © 2019 by Terry Spear

Cover Copyright © 2019 by Terry Spear

Discover more about Terry Spear at:

http://www.terryspear.com/

To Doni Miller, thanks for loving my books and my cover art!! You made my day!

FOREWORD

Synopsis

Ricky Jones is looking forward to his first day on the job as a deputy sheriff in the cougar-run town of Yuma Town, but he doesn't expect to run into his former girlfriend while he's wearing his cougar coat. Now he wants her back in the worst way, but he's sure she's going to be even madder at him for dumping her three years ago.

Mandy Richards is on her way to an interview at a hospital north of Yuma Town for the position of a Licensed Practical Nurse when she hits a cougar in the thick foggy night, a full moon silhouetted in the gloom on Friday, the thirteenth. Checking on the wounded cougar changes her world forever.

But her most recent ex-boyfriend isn't going along with Ricky's plans to renew his relationship and things are bound to turn deadly.

1

Heading from Durango, Colorado to a hospital in Loveland where Mandy Richards had an interview for a job to be a Licensed Practical Nurse, she squinted at the road, barely visible in the thick fog cloaking the entire area. A shadow of something crossed the road, the third time in twenty minutes, but she suspected it was just her imagination. Her right tires spun on gravel, warning her she was on the shoulder again. She swerved back onto the road, glad she hadn't met anyone else driving this way. Her skin crawled with a rash of fresh goosebumps. She had to drive so slowly it had taken her an extra hour to get this far. She should have left Durango earlier. At least she had a hotel reserved in Loveland for the night so she could do her interview first thing in the morning.

A full moon surrounded in fog hung high above the golden aspen and made Friday, the thirteenth, seem even spookier. It was already six and the sun had set. Mandy glanced at her gas gauge. Less than a quarter of a tank. She'd stop for gas in Yuma Town. She should be getting there soon, she thought.

Smiling, she took a deep breath and let it out, thrilled about the prospect of working in Loveland as an LPN and getting away from her boyfriend, if the interview at the hospital she wanted to work at turned out okay. This would be her first real job out of training, and she sure hoped she'd get the position.

The leaves were already turning red and gold and orange in the chilly September weather. She loved this time of year.

She stretched, trying to relax the tension in her muscles, her eyes still straining to see the road. She took a deep breath and sighed and swore she saw something move across the road again. She hit her brakes, but she figured she had to be imagining seeing phantom creatures running in front of her headlights, the gloom making it impossible to really make anything out. Tightening her hands around the steering wheel, she loved the fog when she was at home, not so much when she was driving in the dark on unfamiliar roads. Her headlights were unable to penetrate the gloom, some of the light reflecting back to her, making the visibility worse. She should be nearing Yuma Town soon when she thought she saw something rather big race across the road in front of her.

Her heart in her throat, she slammed on her brakes but too late. Whatever it was, it wasn't a phantom this time and she felt a thud and sent whatever it was flying onto the shoulder of the road. Her heart pounding, she immediately stopped the car.

Was it an animal? A dog, maybe. It couldn't have been a person. She thought it was running too fast and too low to the ground to have been human. She hesitated to get out of the car, afraid it was a wounded dog that could be vicious because of its injuries, not that she would blame him, if that's what it was. She had to make sure she hadn't run into a person or someone's beloved pet. She couldn't leave him injured on the side of the road. She had to see what it was and try to get help for it.

"Nice, doggy," she said, getting out of the car and heading around the front bumper, the headlights illuminating her, her car phone out so she could use the light to see what she'd hit. "Ohmigod." Not a dog. A cougar was lying on its side and he, or she, looked dead, his eyes closed, and he wasn't stirring.

She felt bad that she'd killed the animal, her eyes blurring with tears. She must have blinded him with her headlights, and she hadn't seen him in the thick fog until it was too late. She moved closer to check on it, wanting to see if it had a pulse. What was she thinking? She was a nurse, sure, but not an animal doctor. Even if she were one, this was a wild animal, not a domesticated pet. Still, she drew closer to it, trying to see if it was breathing at all, before she called animal control, if they had one anywhere near Yuma Town.

The cougar stirred, lifting his head so suddenly she didn't have time to react, and he growled and snapped at her, catching her outstretched hand. She shrieked and dropped her car keys next to his head as his wicked teeth dug into her skin, but he just as quickly released her as if he'd thought better of eating her for dinner tonight.

He was probably too injured. She jumped back, favoring her hand. She should never have drawn that close to the wild animal. How was she going to get her car keys back now? No way could she try to grab them that close to those wicked teeth.

His beautiful brown eyes were fluorescent in the light of her cell phone. He almost looked docile and innocent as he watched her, lifting his head slightly. He groaned, laying his head back on the pavement.

Shivering in the thirty-four-degree weather when she was wearing just a sweater, leggings, and boots, her coat sitting in the passenger seat, she stared openmouthed at the big cat and started to back away to the driver's side of the car, favoring her injured hand. Her breath came out in a frosty mist and she saw his breath slightly also. What if he was rabid?

Even if he wasn't, she'd could still get an infection from the bite. Her hand throbbing, she finally reached the car and jumped in, slamming the door, and searched on her phone to call animal control.

She was shaking so hard from the cold, the bite, and feeling so nauseous, she couldn't type on her phone to do a Google search and just called 911 instead.

"What is your emergency?" the Yuma Town Sheriff's Department dispatcher, Amy Mayflower asked.

"I...I hit a cougar on the highway just out of Yuma Town. He or she's not dead, just injured. And I...he...bit me. I...I don't feel well. I...I'd drive into town, but I dropped my keys by the cougar and I...I can't get them."

"I'm sending help out your way right now," the operator said, trying to keep her voice even, but she sounded really concerned anyway, which made Mandy worry even more. Did they know of a rabid cougar in the area? She envisioned a cougar biting half the population of the pets and people in Yuma Town and the cycle repeated as the animals bit others—like a rabid cougar apocalypse. "Just stay on the line," the 911 operator said, interrupting Mandy's morbid thoughts.

She had been sure the operator would make her call another number and she was feeling so lightheaded and not herself that she was glad the woman was taking the necessary steps to get her help. Mandy hoped she was getting aid for the cougar too. She hoped they didn't put him—or her—down. She loved all animals, even if it was a wild cougar that had bitten her. She knew he was only scared and trying to protect himself the only way that he could. But if he was rabid...

Ricky Jones hadn't ever been superstitious before, though his brother Kolby had told him that he was lucky he wasn't working his first day as a deputy sheriff for Sheriff Dan Steinacker in Yuma Town on Friday, the thirteenth, during the full moon. He'd never expected anything like *this* to happen to him. All he'd wanted to do was take a nice long cougar run in the fog, so wrapped up in his thoughts about his first day on the job tomorrow, he hadn't been paying attention to the only car approaching on the road.

Worse, what were the odds that the car was being driven by his ex-girlfriend and she would actually run into him—with her car. Sure, if she knew he was her ex, she'd probably have wanted to. What a mess. Her keys were sitting next to his head, that was splitting in two. He could barely lift his head without blacking out. His leg was broken, he was pretty sure, as much as it was hurting. So much for starting his first day on the job tomorrow. He wanted to carry her keys to the car, leave them for her, then hide in the brush, so she'd feel safe to leave and he'd be safer, in a way. Except he needed medical attention. Since cougar shifters healed in half the time that humans did, he needed to have his bones set before they began to knit together wrong. He was also afraid he'd shift due to the trauma his body was experiencing. Sometimes that would happen. Then he'd be lying there in the cold, naked.

Shooting pains streaked up his leg and he groaned again.

Nothing could be worse than the fact he'd bitten Mandy, drawn blood even, the coppery taste still in his mouth.

Everyone in the shifter community would want to kill him! They were never to reveal to a human what they were, firstly. And they were never to bite another human, which could lead to them turning into one of their own. He still wasn't sorry he had turned his brother. What would Kolby have done without him, when they'd already lost both their parents and all they had was each other? And the reporter, Carl Nelson, had shot Ricky when he was a cougar, so he was fair game. Plus, Kolby had bitten Carl also, so maybe it was his bite and not Ricky's that had turned him.

Man, if Ricky had thought Mandy would be angry at seeing him now, after the breakup three years earlier, she was sure to be pissed at him when she turned into a cougar. If she did. And it was all his fault. With the way his luck was going—reminding himself about the notion that it *was* Friday, the thirteenth—she *would* turn. Guaranteed.

He had a very noble reason for dumping her earlier. At least he could explain the reason for leaving her like he did. The other part? About being a cougar? About biting her? About turning her? That was going to take a little more explaining.

Seeing her brought all the memories he'd shared with her back to life—going to the movies, taking trips to the lake, hiking, study time, just talking, and attending steampunk conventions with her, both of them dressed for the occasion.

Her hand had swept through her dark blond hair, naturally highlighted with golds from the sun, whipped around in the chilly breeze, and her green eyes pierced him to the depth of his soul before she backed away to the safety of her car and got in and shut the door. He so wanted to talk to her, to tell her that he still really cared about her and wanted to get back together with her.

Sirens were headed his way—an ambulance's, Sheriff Dan's, Deputy Sheriffs Hal Haverton, and Chase Buchanan's vehicles too. He even heard Doc Kate Parker-Hill's car's engine. They probably had gotten ahold of the alert roster call-up and were trying to learn which cougar was unaccounted for. *Him.*

Ricky was certain Mandy had told them she'd been bitten and then they would really be worried she'd turn and take off for the woods. They'd definitely be angry with him. If he were a dog, he'd be in the doghouse about now.

In the past, once he no longer was an informant, he knew

there was no getting back together again with her, not because he wouldn't have loved to, but because once he'd been turned, he couldn't see her. Then he smiled a little. Now she was one of them. Maybe.

Then he frowned. She would probably hate his guts for doing this to her. He wondered what she was doing around this area. Maybe she'd learned he was living here and wanted to come see him.

Nah, that was too much to hope for.

He now saw the flashing lights of the emergency vehicles as they approached, and he was glad help was on its way.

Mandy's car door suddenly opened, and he wondered what she was doing. Why would she leave her vehicle when a dangerous cougar lay a few feet from her car? Help would soon arrive. She didn't need to go anywhere.

Then he heard a low growl. Oh. No.

He saw her beautiful cougar face, reddish tanned fur, black markings and white under her chin, right before she tore off across the road, disappearing into the woods and the fog, limping slightly with her right paw. The hand that *he'd* bitten when she'd been human. He felt awful about it.

He struggled to get up, to run after her, to pin her down until help could arrive to take care of her. But he couldn't even sit up, his head and leg hurt so bad. He thought of shifting and hollering for her to stop, but he didn't believe she would. If anything, she'd think he was human, and he wouldn't understand that she was a cougar now.

All the vehicles slowed down as they approached her car and parked. He heard everyone moving toward him, footsteps hurried as they rounded he car, spotlights sweeping the area while searching for him, not knowing yet that they would have to chase her down too.

Man, was he in trouble.

2

Mandy had to be hallucinating. Did rabies victims hallucinate? As far as she recalled from her nurse's training, victims would have a tingling, itching sensation around the bite area. Hers burned and ached like crazy. No tingling or itching. Flu-like symptoms would follow: fever, headaches, nausea, tiredness. She still might feel that way, if it took a little longer to come on. Though she was suffering from the nausea already.

But hallucinations? She hadn't remembered anything in her nurse's training about that. The icy wind blew in her eyes as she ran as a long-legged furry critter, but she was warm at least. Still, she couldn't believe all this seemed so real when she knew she had to be hallucinating.

The sirens were wailing, getting closer to her car. So why was she running away? Through the woods? She needed help for her injured hand. Maybe she needed rabies shots.

No. No. They'd find her passed out in her car and take care of her and do what they had to with the cougar. And get her car keys back to her.

"WHERE'S the woman who was driving the car?" Sheriff Dan asked, looking inside Mandy's car. "Ah hell, she's gone." He ran to join Ricky, his dark brown hair ruffled in the breeze, his blue eyes narrowed with concern. "Ricky. How are you—you have blood on your mouth. You bit the woman, she told the dispatcher. Shift. Tell us where you hurt."

Chase, Hal, and Deputy Sheriff Stryker Hill joined them. Stryker must have ridden with someone else because Ricky hadn't heard his car's engine. Doc Kate and the EMTs reached them after that. They were a welcome sight. Every one of them.

Ricky struggled to shift, his body warming all at once and as soon as he was in his human state, he groaned out, "I think I have a broken leg. And, yeah, I bit my girlfriend."

They moved him onto a stretcher and stabilized his leg and his head, then wrapped him in a blanket.

"You've bashed your head too," Kate said, her red hair hanging over her shoulders as she examined him, like she'd just fallen out of bed, which meant she'd already gone home from work and let loose her beautiful hair. "Let's get him into the ambulance. What about the woman you bit? Where is she?"

"She ran off into the woods." Ricky's skull splitting in two, he closed his eyes. "Yeah. As a cougar."

"All right, get him into the ambulance and take care of him, Doc," Dan said. "The rest of you? We're on a cougar hunt."

"Don't hurt her," Ricky said. "She's my girlfriend. Mandy Richards."

Doc arched a red brow. "An old girlfriend?"

"She's my age."

Doc smiled. "I meant that she was your girlfriend before you arrived in Yuma Town."

"Yeah."

"Is that why you bit her?" Doc asked, as the EMTs loaded Ricky into the ambulance.

Everyone else was supposed to be looking for Mandy but waited to hear what Ricky had to say first.

Not that he didn't have a history of biting someone he cared about so that he could remain friends, but he wouldn't have bitten his ex-girlfriend.

"No. She reached her hand down toward me. I don't know. I was startled, lashing out, just coming to. I...I thought the person meant to kill me, then realized it was Mandy. I couldn't believe she was here. That she ran into me, though I can imagine she would have loved to when I first left her. She'll kill me, now that I've turned her." He let out his breath on a heavy sigh and groaned again.

"We'll get you patched up in no time," Dan said.

"I can't work tomorrow. I've messed everything up." Ricky felt terrible about it. He was so eager to work at his new job, to prove to the other guys that he could be more than an informant or a ranch hand, but he had really gone and done it this time.

Dan shook his head and patted his shoulder. "You can work in the office while your leg is casted. No problem at all. And about Mandy, we'll take care of her."

Stryker and Chase had already shifted and growled to let them know they were headed into the woods.

"Come on, Hal. Let's get going so Doc can take care of Ricky." Dan headed off for the woods; Hal hurried after him.

The ambulance took off for the clinic and every bump in the road made Ricky's leg and head hurt. Ricky was already wondering what they were going to do with Mandy once they caught up to her. She would have trouble controlling her shifting. Why had she come here? What if she *had* known he was living here now and wanted to renew their relationship?

He was hoping so, yet, he figured he'd blown that now.

Where would she stay? He'd have to ask Hal and Tracey if she could stay with them out at the ranch. He smiled a little. Then he frowned. If he was going to work at the sheriff's office now instead of out at the ranch, he'd only see her when he returned home at night.

Still, that was better than nothing and he would have time to convince her that he was still an excellent choice of a boyfriend for her. And more.

∾

MANDY WAS LIVING A NIGHTMARE. Lights were shining this way and that as two men tracked her, but no matter how much she tried to shake them, they followed her like they could smell her trail. Then she saw two cougars flanking her and her heart nearly gave out. They were larger than her and she suspected they were males.

A couple of vehicles headed out on the road where she'd come from. Did they save the cougar? She hadn't heard any gunfire, so she hoped they hadn't shot it. What if they shot her!

But she was hallucinating. Or caught up in a night terror, nightmare paralysis, or effect from the bite that she couldn't shake loose of.

"Mandy! Mandy Richards!" one of the men shouted.

Okay, now she really knew this was all a horrible figment of her imagination. No one here knew her name. Well, besides the fact that they wouldn't be calling out to her as if she were running as a human.

"We don't want to hurt you. Just stop running from us. We'll take care of your injury and explain what's going on. Your boyfriend, Ricky Jones, didn't mean to bite you."

Her heart was already racing went into overdrive. She hadn't thought about him in forever. Well, that wasn't quite true. She often wondered what had become of him. But here, in this place, with her new life ahead of her, new town, new makeover, she was leaving her old life behind, and for the moment, she hadn't been thinking about him. He bit her? A cougar bit her!

How would they know she had dated Ricky? Maybe she was in a coma. Maybe they had read her driver's license and knew her name that way. And she was hearing bits and pieces of conversation that drifted into her coma-like state. No way would they know who she had dated in the past though. Unless... unless she had mentioned him in her confusion and hadn't even realized she'd said anything. Why wouldn't she have said Edgar Sanderson's name? The guy she'd been dating, until she tried to call it quits? He should have been the one on her mind.

"Okay, we'll take her down that way."

Down? Like "shooting her" taking her down?

Then she heard a shot fired, a stab in her flank, and she stumbled, fell, collapsed. Okay, so they caught her, all right? She could end this nightmare now and wake up or sleep more soundly.

One of the men lifted her in his arms and started carrying her back the way she'd come. At least she thought so.

"You don't think Ricky did this on purpose, do you, Dan?" the guy carrying her asked.

"No, Hal. I believe he was telling the truth, that it was an accident." His hair dark and his expression darker, Dan said, "Hey, Stryker, Chase, you can meet us at the clinic. Since the two of you came in the same car, maybe one of you can take her car there. I'll carry Mandy in my car and see you in a few."

The two cougars that were still flanking them both growled and ran off. The other men were dressed in jeans, jackets, cowboy boots and hats, and she'd seen one of them wearing a badge. She suspected they were with a sheriff's office, rather than from a police station.

"Hal, can you take her in at your ranch after she's feeling better? Since she's Ricky's girlfriend and you and Tracey have had experience dealing with newly turned cougars?" Dan asked.

Hal's dark brown eyes considered her, as if trying to decide if she was a safe bet or not.

Now Mandy was certain this was perfectly unreal. It was just all part of a crazy, mixed-up nightmare because of running into the cougar and then him biting her.

"I'll have to talk to Tracey about it, but yeah, I'm sure she'll be agreeable."

Mandy was fighting falling asleep, or she should say a deeper sleep where she wouldn't be having such a real dream. Then she wondered why. When she woke, she'd be her normal self, her hand bandaged, antibiotics administered, and as long as she didn't have rabies, she was heading to Loveland as planned. Unless they put her on pain medication to deal with her aching hand. Shouldn't they have already? If they had, it wasn't working.

Then she dropped off completely and she didn't have any more dreams.

"I want to see her," Ricky told Elsie Miller, his nurse. She wore scrubs featuring colorful dragons on a blue and gold starred background, her typical style—bright, cheerful, and fun. He swore she had a really stern side when it came to him obeying the clinic rules, but she also had a soft side when it came to her patients.

"I told you already, you hit your head hard and Doc Kate said no moving from the bed, until tomorrow, except for going to the bathroom and you call one of us before you leave the bed. We'll make sure you get there all right. Besides, you're on pain medication and we don't want you falling and breaking the other leg or something else. Doc Kate is going home soon and Dr. Rugel will be coming in to cover emergencies for the night."

Kolby walked into the room, smiled at the nurse, and frowned at Ricky, his blue eyes worried. He ran his hands through his hair, blonder than Ricky's. "Hey, bro, are you going to be okay?"

"You and your brother are two of our worst patients," the nurse said, smiled, and left them alone to visit.

"Yeah, I've got a broken leg and a mild concussion. You won't believe who ran into me."

"In this fog? I can imagine anybody could be at fault if you were foolish enough to cross the road in your cougar coat."

"Mandy Richards."

Kolby's jaw hung agape.

"Yeah, *my* Mandy Richards."

"From Durango?" As if there would be another one in the whole state of Colorado.

"Yeah. She's going to be so pissed off at me."

"Why? She ran into *you*. Unless you dented her car."

"I bit her."

Kolby's eyes grew round, then he cast him a small smile. "Déjà vu."

"I didn't bite her for the same reason I bit you," Ricky said, perturbed. "I don't make it a habit of biting people. Just you. Well, and Carl Nelson, but we both bit him."

"He deserved it. He had already shot you and was trying to kill you." Kolby grabbed a chair and pulled it closer to the bed. "So that's why you said she would be pissed off at you, more than she already would be because you had dumped her without telling her why." Before Ricky could defend himself, Kolby raised his hand. "*We* all know why. Except she doesn't."

"Have you seen her yet? I should have asked Elsie if they'd

brought her in yet. She didn't say whether or not she was here. Just that I can't leave the bed. I wondered if she was still a cougar."

Kolby shook his head. "I didn't know you turned anyone before I got here. Let alone that it was your old girlfriend. You get yourself into the worst messes."

"They could put her in the same room as me and that would save up a room for someone else, if someone else needed it."

"Are you kidding? Once she learns what happened to her and you were the cause of it? I can just imagine a cat fight, except with you in your cast, you wouldn't be shifting, and you'd be sporting some big-toothed cat bites, along with your broken leg and banged-up head."

"I want to see her. I want to explain to her why I had left her."

"I'm sure you'll have plenty of time to do that."

They heard someone's footsteps coming down the hall and Ricky tensed, unable to help himself.

Dan came into the room and shook his head. "Mandy's asleep in bed. She shifted but didn't wake. Elsie told me you want to see her, but you aren't to leave the bed, according to Doc Kate. And Doc William will be apprized of the situation, so no disobeying the rules. I know you want to see her first and explain something about what's going on and apologize to her, but you both need a little time to recuperate. Tomorrow, if the doc says you're well enough to leave your bed, you can. In the meantime, get some rest."

"What about my working tomorrow?" Ricky was still afraid Dan would decide he was too impulsive or reckless to hire him and would fire him before he even had a chance to work one day on the job.

Dan sighed. "Let's leave it up to the doctors. If they say you're ready to work, you can come into the office. I don't want you driving until you're cleared for it completely. We've got things covered otherwise."

Ricky must have looked so down about it—you know, the part about how they really didn't need him because they got it covered—that Dan added, "But we're not letting you off the hook. Not after all the training we sent you through."

"Where is she going to live?" Ricky blurted out, now that his job wasn't in jeopardy, for the moment.

"Hal is going to talk to Tracey about her moving in with them. Of course, she won't be living in the bunkhouse with you and Kolby and Ted. But you can see her when you're not working and try to renew your friendship. Tracey has to agree though. With you and your brother, they had ranch foreman, Ted Weekum, to watch over the two of you while you got your shifting under control. But Tracey and Hal work, and they've got four three-year-olds now, so it's a little different."

"I'll watch over her." Ricky was eager to help her transition into her new way of life.

"You'll be working," Dan reminded him.

"Uh, yeah, but when I'm not."

"If she will even speak to you," Kolby reminded him.

"Uh, yeah, well there's that." But Ricky was persistent when he wanted something. And right now, he really wanted to see her. "I want to order some flowers for her."

Dan chuckled. "I'm out of here."

Kolby was smiling when he shook his head, pulled his phone out of his pocket, and called a florist.

ACCORDING to the clock on the wall, it was the middle of the night and Mandy was lying in a bed, her wrists confined to the railings as if she were a common criminal. Why? Because she'd run into a cougar? It wasn't like she had hit a person and taken off, leaving the injured person behind. And she had been injured by the cat. She looked at her hand and saw that it was wrapped in bandages. She was wearing an IV and she suspected they were giving her antibiotics to fight infection. The call button was near her hand and she was torn about pushing it and finding out just why she'd been confined to the bed or let the nurse on duty rest. She was more sympathetic to their cause now that she was one too.

She frowned. Did she have rabies? And that's why they had her confined to the bed? Great. Just great. Note to self: if she hit another wild animal, she was not getting near it. Then she noticed a dozen red roses and carnations filling a vase on a nearby table.

Well, that was nice, anyway. She didn't think they could be from Edgar. He didn't know where she was going, and as far as she knew, she hadn't told anyone else about him. The more she eyed them, the more she wanted to know who they were from. But she wasn't going to call the on-duty nurse just to learn that bit of information.

Then she heard someone approaching the room, but not in a regular way. Not on one footstep after another. She couldn't make out the sound. Then Ricky appeared in the doorway of her room. Ricky Jones. His dark brown hair shorter than she'd remembered it, his dark brown eyes considering her for a moment.

Her mouth agape, she couldn't believe he was standing there in a hospital gown, his head bandaged, his leg in a cast and he was on crutches.

"What are you doing here?" she asked.

"Shhh, I'll be in trouble if they learn I left my room. I just had to see you and to know you are going to be all right."

"Come in and close the door then."

He did and sat in a chair that was across the room. "I'd move it closer, but I'm not really able. When the swelling goes down, they're putting me in a walking cast. What are you doing here?"

"I was on my way to Loveland to interview for a position of an LPN at a hospital but was going to stop in here to get some gas. Then I hit a cougar and he or she bit me. I think they believe I have rabies." Mandy raised her hands to show she was confined. "What happened to you?"

"I, uh, live here. Listen, Mandy, before I say anything else, I have to tell you why I left you in Durango the way that I did."

"It's water under the bridge. I moved on. I'm in a relationship with someone new." Though as far as she was concerned, that relationship was over for her, but she didn't feel she needed to explain that to Ricky.

"Who?" Ricky sounded shocked to hear it, which annoyed her.

"Oh, for heaven's sake, you left me. What did you expect? For me to wait around for you to change your mind?" She'd never really gotten over him, but she had no plans to get back together with him either, just because she ran into him here at the clinic.

He slumped in his chair and looked miserable.

"So, what was the reason that you left me?" She wanted to hear whatever story she figured he was going to make up.

"I was serving as an informant for a couple of different law enforcement agencies. Things were getting really hairy and I couldn't involve you. A couple of the guys were friends of Kolby's but he didn't know they were bad guys. Anyway, I couldn't tell you why I left. It was better that you had no clue about where I'd gone."

"You were an informant?" She couldn't believe how dangerous his situation could have been. It was hard for her to believe he would have done something like that. Then again, when it came to protecting his only other living relative, his brother, she could understand that. And she had to admit he had been protecting her too.

"Yeah. Both of the agents live here in Yuma Town now, and well, it's a long story, but I helped them put away some bad guys. Honey, the former informant, had been murdered. I took his place. You can see why I didn't want you involved."

"Murdered?" She stared at him for a moment in surprise, her heartbeat thumping harder, and she shook her head. "I...I thought you were seeing someone else. Or maybe that you had returned home to Cody, Wyoming where you and your brother were from." She'd been born there too but was never going back. She couldn't believe how wrong she'd been about him.

"Not me. There's never been anyone like you for me. I had to do the job I did to protect my brother, but I didn't want to give you up. I just didn't have any choice if I was going to keep you safe." Then he glanced at the vase of flowers and smiled. "Do you like your roses?"

"They're from you?" That surprised her too, but she shouldn't have been. He'd been sensitive about her needs, until he dumped her. But if he'd done so to keep her from getting hurt, she had to rethink how she'd been feeling concerning his leaving her so long ago.

"Yeah."

"Thanks. They're lovely." She motioned with her head toward him. "How did you get injured?"

"You ran into me with your car."

3

R icky was all set to explain about Mandy hitting him with her car when he was running across the road as a cougar, figuring it was going to take some convincing that he and the cougar were the same, when the door opened to Mandy's room and the nurse on duty, Marcus Jones, unrelated to Ricky's brother and him, peered in at him. "You weren't supposed to be out of bed. Doctor's orders."

"I—"

"Out, or I'll wake Doc William and he'll order a sedative for you so you'll stay in bed."

"I have a mild concussion," Ricky said to Mandy, touching his bandaged head lightly, wanting her to know that it wasn't just his broken leg they were concerned about. If that's all it had been, he would have gone home already.

"You didn't tell me that." Mandy tilted her chin down in a way that said she couldn't believe he'd disobey his doctor.

He smiled. "I'll talk to you in the morning." He wished Marcus hadn't stopped what he was going to say to Mandy about being a cougar. But he was glad he was finally able to tell her about why he'd had to end their relationship before someone he was informing on learned of her and killed her.

He hobbled back down the hallway and resettled in his bed, Marcus hovering over him until he made sure he wasn't going anywhere else.

"You could just move her in here with me," Ricky said.

"The doctor would have to okay that, and Miss Richards would have to be agreeable. Besides, you know she's newly turned, and we never know how someone will react. She could shift, be confused, and hurt you. Especially because you turned her in the first place. Go to sleep." Marcus turned out his lights. "We'll see you in the morning unless you need something else before then."

"I'm good. Thanks."

Then Marcus nodded and left his room.

Ricky knew he had to sleep, but he sure wanted to return to Mandy's room and tell her about this cougar business, not wanting any more secrets between them. Then he remembered what she'd told him about the new boyfriend. Well, the only thing good about any of this was maybe he could repair the damage between them, and her boyfriend would be out of the picture, especially because she was now one of them. But the other thing was that she couldn't work as an LPN for a hospital in Loveland. He just hoped they'd considered hiring her to work here. But she'd have to take time to get her shifting under control.

He finally dropped off to sleep until he felt something large sitting on top of him on his hospital bed and his eyes popped open. There, sitting on his legs was one ferocious-looking cougar—female variety, her green eyes fluorescent in the hallway's light seeping into his room.

~

MANDY COULDN'T BELIEVE she was a were-cougar. What other explanation could there be? The cougar bit her. She was having nightmares about being a cougar, and now she was wide awake and a cougar again? It was the only way she could get out of her restraints that had confined her to the hospital bed. Big paws and skinny wrists, much easier to maneuver with and slip out of the restraints than it had been with her hands.

She had smelled Ricky's scent when he'd been in her room and followed it to his room, which was something she'd never been able to do before. Her kitty cat paws had silently padded along the hallway not alerting anyone she was out and about, something that was new to her too.

Ricky had been sleeping soundly, looking angelic, for him. He had a fun devilish side to him, a little reckless when she was never that way and that had always fascinated her about him.

She felt a little guilty confronting him like this when he could be really badly injured. But if she hadn't been hallucinating before, and this was all for real now, she wanted to know if he truly had been the cougar that had bitten her.

Bits and pieces of conversations had all come crashing back to her when she woke from a deep sleep and found she was a cougar again: that she had hit Ricky with her car, that he had bitten her, that she'd been turned, that others—a Hal and Tracey—would take her in because they'd taken care of the brothers who had been newly turned.

Now, she was sitting on Ricky's thighs, giving him the evil cat eye, waiting for him to wake up enough to tell her the truth.

His lips parted in surprise, but he didn't scream out in terror, which meant he had to be a cougar, right? Or he would have been terrified to see a cougar sitting on top of him. He clamped his mouth shut. He'd better not reach for the nurse's call button.

He let out his breath finally. "I tried to explain to you earlier what had happened between us when Marcus made me return to my bed. I'm so sorry, Mandy. If I could undo what I did, I would. I didn't mean to bite you. I was just coming to, and I saw your hand reaching toward me and I panicked, thinking whoever you were would injure me worse. As soon as I snapped at you, meaning only to get you to back off and not hurt me, I realized I'd gotten too close to your hand and had actually bitten you. I swear I didn't mean to. As soon as I was focusing better—my head was splitting in two and my vision blurring—I realized it was you. Mandy. My girlfriend."

She softly snarled.

"Part of me hoped you had learned I was living in Yuma Town and had come to see me. The realistic side of me said you were just passing through and it was fate. I was in terrible pain though."

He took a deep breath and rubbed his head. She wondered if he was still hurting and she thought maybe he should have more pain medication.

"I wanted you to come and join me in here so we could talk. Marcus said you probably wouldn't want to be in the same room as me after you learned I'd bitten you. But I wanted to tell you it's not all bad, you know."

She growled.

"Really. It isn't. We heal much more quickly. I bet you're healing much faster than you would as a human right now."

She had to admit her injured hand was starting to itch and tingle, just like the symptoms for rabies. But if it was just healing, then that was a good sign.

"We heal in half the time it takes humans to heal. My leg will mend in about three to four weeks instead of six to eight weeks. Your hand should be completely healed in just a few days."

She could definitely get onboard with that.

"Your hearing and sense of smell are vastly improved if you wondered how you could smell me and hear so much that's going on when before you couldn't. The light's turned out in the room and yet you can see me as though it was daylight out. Which proves you can see better in the dark. It's great. Just think, you don't have to have a flashlight in the dark. You don't even have to turn on your lights at home if you get up and wander around at night if you don't want to."

That could be useful, she had to admit.

"The downside, of course, is that you don't have a lot of control over shifting at first."

Oh, just great. What about her job interview tomorrow? She could just envision having the urge to shift on the way to Loveland and having to pull the car onto the shoulder of the road and park, strip out of her clothes, and turn into a cougar. What if someone saw her and hunted her?

This was totally unreal. She hoped she'd be released from the clinic early tomorrow and she would still make it in time for her job interview. If this was still all some crazy nightmare.

"We don't just shift when the full moon is out, like the old werewolf lore. You can shift at any time that you want. Well, it will take you a while to learn how to get your shifting under control. I'm really sorry," Ricky said. "I'll do anything to make it up to you."

Undo it?

"Oh, and we can move really quietly, as you might have noticed, can run long distances, even if you're not used to running, and can climb trees." He smiled. "Leap into them actually from a long way down below too."

They heard footsteps and she turned to look at the doorway, her heart beating spastically—the notion someone would call the police and have her shot—instantly coming to mind.

Marcus peered in, turned on the light, and frowned. "What in the world are you doing in here?" he asked Mandy, as if she could answer him, and then he turned to Ricky. "Are you okay?"

Mandy growled. Was Ricky okay? What about her? She guessed the nurse had worried she'd want to tear into Ricky for doing what he'd done to her. But didn't he look perfectly fine? She glanced at his bandaged head. Well, maybe not. And she did do that to him.

"Okay, look, what do you want to do?" Marcus folded his arms while he looked sternly at Mandy. "Stay in here with Ricky? Or return to your bed for the rest of the night? No matter what, you've got to get off Ricky."

She growled at Marcus, leapt off Ricky, and landed on the floor so quietly, she was amazed, then headed for the door where Marcus wisely moved out of her path. "Do you need anything, Ricky?"

"More pain medication, if I can have some."

"For your head? Or your leg?"

Mandy paused in the hall to hear his answer.

"Both."

That worried her that his head was still hurting. She wanted to know if they had done a CT scan for him. She snorted. A CAT scan. The good thing was he seemed lucid and didn't seem to have forgotten anything, like being struck by her car, or who she was. He seemed to know the clinic staff.

Then she worried that maybe when they were cougars, they didn't fully have control over their wild animal behavior—like the old movie *Wolfman* where the man turned into a wolf and killed people randomly. She wondered if she looked just like a real cougar, and not some deranged were-cougar. Then again, if she looked anything like what Ricky did when he was a cougar —though she still couldn't believe he could be the one she hit on the road—he looked just like a real cougar. She needed to see her whole self in a mirror.

The issue with not being able to control the wild cougar part probably wasn't true, since Ricky had explained he'd just reacted because he thought he was protecting himself and had been injured so badly. Any animal would have reacted in much the same way. As annoyed as she'd been that Ricky had turned her, she hadn't had any interest in biting him. Or Marcus, for giving her grief either.

She reached her room and leaped onto the hospital bed but hadn't judged the power of her jump and landed clear on the other side, knocking over her table, the flowers, a pitcher of water and a cup with a clatter of humongous proportions. She hoped nobody else was trying to sleep here tonight. If she'd been in her human form, she would have laughed. She tried again and this time she managed to jump right onto the center of the bed. It looked like this was going to take some practice though. She could imagine trying to leap into a tree and missing the branch completely. She hoped to get some practice in while no one was watching.

Marcus hurried into the room, saw she was lying on the bed and sighed. "When I took this job, I never expected to be dealing with newly turned cougars. We could send you to the vet clinic."

And put her in a cage? Those were fighting words.

4

Early the next morning, Ricky woke to find Mandy pacing across his room. "Good, you're awake," she said, frowning at him. "I need to get out of here. I have a job interview in Loveland. I wanted to see you before I go and tell you I'm not angry with you for biting me. Any wild animal would have done what you did. I'll...I'll deal with this like I would anything else in my life."

Ricky sighed. He understood how she was feeling. Her world had turned upside down and it would never be the same. At least he knew all about it, unlike those who were born as shifters. But it would most likely take some time before she could have some control over shifting into her cougar. And it was going to be difficult for her to understand that right away.

"It's going to be a while before you can get your shifting under control. It can take months." Years even, but he didn't want to tell her that. Hopefully, she'd learn quickly. "You'll need to stay with our kind. Yuma Town is cougar shifter run. So you'll be safe here. Everyone will understand if you have to shift all of a sudden. Tracey and Hal Haverton have a horse ranch and they're going to take you in. I think. I live there in the bunkhouse for now, but I'm a deputy sheriff and not a ranch hand any longer. Though I'll help out on my days off."

"You know how to ride a horse?"

"Yeah. Break them. Take care of them. Even help with foaling."

"Where was I supposed to stay? The bunkhouse too?"

"No, my brother and I and Ted Weekum, the ranch foreman, stay at the bunkhouse. You would stay in the main house. I have to warn you Hal and Tracey Haverton have four three-year-olds."

"Wait, oh, no, don't tell me. Were-cougars have multiple births like their wild halves have."

"Were-cougars? We're cougar shifters. Don't believe anything you've read or seen about shifters. But yeah, most everyone has a couple of kids or more at a time."

Dr. Kate came into the room. "Here you are. I was going to discharge you this morning into Tracey Haverton's care. She said she'd be happy to take you in and talk to you about everything you want to ask about and more. But I wanted to see how you're feeling first."

"My hand feels better, but the rest of this?" Mandy waved her hand at herself. "The rest of this I'm not sure about at all."

"You'll get used to it. Just like the brothers did. I'm sure they'll both help you through this also, having been there and done it too."

"I have a job interview."

The doctor's face fell, and Mandy knew she couldn't go to it. She felt terrible about it. All she wanted to do was be a nurse. Then the doctor smiled and patted her shoulder. "We'll make sure you're gainfully employed as soon as you can control your shifting. Do you have any training in some field?"

"I'm an LPN."

Kate's jaw dropped, then she recovered and smiled. "See?

You're in just the right place. You're hired. As soon as you can control your shifting. If you don't mind helping with Tracey's toddlers, or helping out at the ranch in some other way, then we'll be all set for when you can come to work for us here."

Tracey walked into the room and introduced herself. Ricky was so glad they were not only taking her in at the ranch, but that Dr. Kate was hiring her too. He hoped that Mandy would feel better about everything then and that she still didn't have her heart set on working in Loveland.

"When can I leave?" Ricky wanted to go where Mandy was going as if he were a lovesick pup.

Dr. Kate said, "No more headaches?"

"No, I'm fine."

"Okay, but if you start feeling poorly—"

"Mandy's a nurse and she'll get me back here if I need to return."

Kate smiled. "All right then. Mandy, you have your first patient. Make sure he tells you the truth."

Ricky was in a hurry to get out of bed and get dressed.

Tracey said, "We'll wait for you in the lobby. Don't rush. We don't want you falling and breaking something else. Dan's depending on you to get to work soon." Then Tracey and Mandy left the room and the doc handed him his discharge papers.

"Remember, headaches, nausea, feeling dizzy, you let Mandy know right away," Doc said.

"Yes, ma'am."

Then Kate smiled at him. "I thought you only liked the older ladies. Now I know it's because your former girlfriend has some kind of a hold over you, and no one close to her age would do. We'll see you about your leg in about three weeks. Make sure you have an appointment for your cast removal."

"I will. Thanks, Doc."

Then Ricky thought of Mandy's boyfriend, but if she was

moving to Loveland, maybe they weren't sticking together. She couldn't be with him now anyway. Unless she thought to turn him. That was something else they needed to tell her. No turning other people. He was certain he shouldn't be the one telling her that though—not after turning two people, possibly three, already himself.

Still, he wanted to know more about this guy as soon as possible. No way did Ricky want them to get back together, whether they had broken up already or were still in a relationship—even if she hadn't been turned, but especially since she had been. He could just imagine seeing the guy here and her turning him and then they'd be one big happy cougar family in Yuma Town. *Not.*

MANDY REALLY LIKED Dr. Kate Parker-Hill and was grateful she'd given her a job. The thing was that a job at the hospital in Loveland had never been guaranteed. She just hoped she could start working there soon. She'd never taken care of kids much, so she couldn't imagine having to do that. Horses? They were huge and scary.

Taking care of Ricky as his personal nurse? She shook her head. Sure, she would take care of him if he needed her to, professional ethics and all, but he was still her *ex*-boyfriend.

When they were released from the clinic, Mandy was riding up front with Tracey in her car while Ricky was sitting in the back, being really quiet. She knew him well enough to realize he was hoping to get back together with her.

"You can't turn anyone, you know," he suddenly said.

The statement came out of the blue so sudden like it took her by surprise. For a second. And then she gave a sarcastic laugh. "Like you?"

"Yeah, well, I did it by accident."

"With me."

Ricky didn't say anything.

"Why in the world would I bite anyone? Unless I don't have control over it when I shift, I don't see myself doing that, ever," she said.

They were silent for some time as they drove into the country, then Ricky said, "I mean, on purpose. You can't bite anyone on purpose."

"What about your brother?" She understood why he'd want to turn his brother as close as they were and because they had no other family to speak of. Their dad had died in a hunting accident that had led to their mom overdosing on prescription medicines. At last the dad had set up trust funds for the boys so the mother couldn't touch their money to buy more drugs. But they'd always been there for each other. She understood that. She didn't have any family left either. No siblings ever. So why would she want to turn someone?

"That was different," Ricky said.

"Okay, you mean I can't change some human guy I get interested in."

Ricky didn't say anything, and she looked over the seat back to see he was smiling. He quickly lost the smile and she rolled her eyes. She looked out at the beautiful fall colors. Wisps of snow floated down from the heavens.

"Halloween's coming in six weeks," he said, changing the subject.

She didn't respond.

"The cougars have a big Halloween party. Everyone dresses up. Kids and adults. If you have to shift, it's no problem. Kolby and I were dressed in Steampunk duds when we both had to shift last year. We chased the kids around the hall as cougars, making them squeal in delight."

She smiled. She could actually see Ricky doing that. She was a little surprised about Kolby doing that. He was more bookish, had more of a work ethic. Though she guessed Ricky did too, except his idea of a job had been downright dangerous in dealing with the criminals. Now he was going to be a deputy sheriff.

"Do you remember the last time you and I dressed in Steampunk costumes?" he asked.

"Yeah, and the next year, you bugged out on me. I still have my costume. I thought I'd wear it to a Halloween party, if I found one to go to this year."

"Well, great. Now you can go to ours. We have different themes every year. I got to pick it this year, so I opted for a steampunk Halloween."

"How fun. What about humans who attend the party? If I suddenly have to turn?"

"It's strictly by cougar invitation only."

It would make her feel better if she were welcomed to the community, though she could imagine being horribly self-conscious if she shifted during the party. At least for Ricky he had his brother who had been having the same difficulty.

"The two of them—Ricky and Kolby—sure were up to some mischief when they were newly turned," Tracey said.

Mandy smiled. She could see Ricky being like that. "How did you get turned, Ricky?" she asked.

"One of the bad guys I informed on was a cougar and he bit me. So I didn't have a choice."

Oh, how awful. She could imagine how terrified he must have been, and she figured the guy hadn't done it by accident, but to kill him. "What happened to him?"

"He was killed. We don't jail murderous cougars. Not that we had much choice anyway."

"Oh." Now that, she hadn't expected.

"It's a different world for us as cougars. We can't be incarcerated long term for fear that someone can't control their shifting, or because some prisoner makes them angry and the prisoner who is a cougar shifts," Tracey said.

"If you run into any trouble at all, you need to let one of us know about it right away. Like if someone sees you shift, or you accidentally bite a human. Or you're injured and are in a hospital somewhere else where they don't have a cougar medical staff. We heal too quickly. But at least our blood and everything about us is all human or all cougar, no mix of the two if anyone should run tests on you," Ricky said.

"That's good to know." She hadn't even considered that part of the equation yet.

"You planned to move to Loveland if you got a job, right?" Tracey asked.

"Yeah."

"Okay, well, since you have a job here now, as soon as you can shift okay, you must be planning on moving here," Tracey said.

"Uh, yeah, I'll have to do that."

"You'll have tons of help. We just need to know what you need moved and when you want to do it," Tracey said.

"I'll have to go with whoever goes," Mandy said.

"You could shift when it's not a good idea," Ricky said. "But I'll go."

"You have your leg in a cast."

"I'm still going."

"I have a roommate at the apartment, so I want to make sure I only get my things." Mandy really didn't want him going along for the ride. The others, sure, in case Edgar gave her trouble about moving out. But she didn't want Edgar and Ricky getting into it.

"I'm sure she would let us know what is hers and what is yours," Ricky said, sounding adamant about her not going.

"My roommate doesn't know I planned on leaving and he's a guy, not a girl."

"*He*? He's gay, right?" Ricky said.

"No, he's not gay and we've been dating, all right? He wanted to make sure we were compatible before we tied the knot."

"Is there any issue about paying the rent?" Tracey asked, quickly changing the subject. "If you had some agreement that you had to give a couple of months' notice, we'll handle it."

"Thanks, but he was paying the rent. I was volunteering at a hospital until I could work as an LPN."

"But you didn't want to work in Durango," Ricky said, sounding suspicious of her relationship with her boyfriend.

"It wasn't working out, okay? That doesn't mean you and I are getting together again either though."

"Did he want you to leave Durango?" Ricky asked as they parked at the ranch.

When they arrived, Mandy loved the view of the mountains, barns, corrals, and horses, the wide-open spaces, just beautiful. "No. I told him I was doing the interview, but I didn't tell him where I was going. I'm sure he assumed I was going to the interview somewhere locally."

"When did you want to leave Durango?" Tracey asked as they piled out of the car.

"Right away. I might as well get this done, get my clothes and other things, and let him know I'm not staying with him any longer." None of this was going to be easy, moving to a place she hadn't intended, having so many people willing to help her out, when she'd expected to be alone in her new life, dealing with the cougar shifting business. "Aren't the horses afraid of you when they smell you are cougars or see you wearing your cougar fur coat?" Mandy asked Tracey.

"No. We raised them, and they're used to our scent and sight, both as cougars and humans," Tracey said.

Kolby hurried over to greet them. "I still can't believe you bit Mandy and she's not too mad at you that she would stay here with us."

"She's coming to the Halloween party. Doc gave her a job so she's happy," Ricky said.

Mandy scoffed. "Wait until I keep having shifting issues."

"Come inside and I'll show you your room and let you meet the kids and Hal," Tracey said.

Hal was home and had the kids playing with finger paints, his own fingers just as covered with paint. "It's washable," he said, smiling.

"Uh-huh," Tracey said. "Hal wants the kids to explore every artistic avenue to see if any of them have an aptitude in something. His parents were adamant that he'd never be an artist, so he's determined to encourage the kids that they can do anything they set their minds to do." She pointed to each of the kids, "That's Liam with the blue paint on his hands and nose, Evan Chase with the green paint on his shirt, Tabitha with the yellow hands, and Denise who's perfectly clean. This is Mandy Richards and she's staying with us for a while." Then she led Mandy into the guestroom where she would stay.

Ricky followed behind them in his walking cast.

"I think she only meant to show me my room, not you," Mandy said to Ricky.

He gave her one of his winning smiles that had always charmed her. "You're my nurse, so I need to stick close to you, in case I'm in distress."

"Okay, well, as your nurse, I order you to return to the living room and put your foot up. Or go to the bunkhouse and get some sleep. If you have any trouble, Kolby can come and get me."

5

The next day, though Mandy wanted to drive her own car to her shared apartment with Edgar in Durango, Ricky knew she couldn't. Not with the problem she'd have with shifting.

They left early that morning, Hal driving a rental van and Chase driving a Suburban, carrying Mandy and Ricky. Ricky wasn't sure what to expect when they arrived at her apartment and had to deal with the boyfriend, though he, Chase, and Hal were wearing deputy sheriff badges, jeans, jackets, and cowboy boots and they were armed. Unfortunately, Ricky was wearing a walking cast on his left leg. They were dressed for trouble in the event Mandy's boyfriend gave them any difficulty.

When they finally reached the apartment, Mandy said, "Edgar's car is here. And that's one of his brothers' cars."

She sounded worried about it. Ricky was glad that Chase and Hal had come with them in case Edgar created a scene. He wished he didn't have a gimpy leg to deal with, or he'd take care of Edgar on his own.

They got out of the vehicles and Mandy said to Ricky, "Are you sure you want to go inside?"

"Yeah, I'm sure. I want to help. I'm not going to beat up the guy if you're worried about that."

She smiled at him. "I was more worried he might hurt you. *I* already hurt you. You don't need to prove anything to him or to me."

"I'll be fine." Ricky was hoping once they got to know each other again, she and he could become more than just friends. He was glad she was getting out of her relationship with this Edgar guy.

Mandy frowned. "I hear his other brother is talking in there also," she warned.

"That shouldn't be a problem," Chase said as they followed her to the apartment, all of them carrying boxes.

Mandy unlocked the door and started inside, Chase and Hal following. Ricky was right behind them, hobbling along, wishing he could have been walking in with Mandy, to show Edgar she was with him, even if she really wasn't.

A blond-haired man with a scraggly beard, immediately got up from the couch where two other men were sitting while they watched TV.

"What the hell is this all about?" the one man said, Ricky assuming it was Edgar.

"I have a job and I'm moving, Edgar. My friends are here to help me." Mandy didn't wait for Edgar to respond and she headed down the hall.

Ricky noted she didn't tell them where she was moving to and he suspected she was worried he'd come after her and cause trouble. But what worried Ricky more was that the men were all cougars.

The man's eyes went round. "You're all cougars. Who the hell did that to you, Mandy?"

"You and your brothers are cougars too?" Mandy appeared as shocked as Ricky felt and she looked ready to collapse.

Ricky quickly grabbed her arm. He didn't blame her. She had been living here with a cougar all along. One who had been turned or was born that way though? He suspected they'd been born that way, or she would have caught them shifting at some time or another.

Edgar made a step in his direction to pull them apart, but Hal and Chase quickly interceded, both showing their badges. Ricky showed his too, since today he was supposed to officially be on the payroll.

"Back off," Chase said to Edgar, his tone dark and menacing. "You don't want to interfere in this."

Ricky again wished he wasn't wearing a darned cast. He wanted to look as lethal as Hal and Chase appeared right now. Instead, he felt useless, though he wore his fiercest expression, but the walking cast ruined his bad-to-the-bone deputy sheriff look. He went with Mandy to help her pack her clothes and everything else she wanted to take with her in her bedroom.

Hal came back to check on them, bringing some boxes, while Chase remained in the living room, keeping the brothers in check.

"I can't believe they're cougars," she said, packing her clothes in a couple of bags while Hal and Ricky packed the rest of her things in boxes.

"Yeah, we were sure surprised too," Hal said.

Ricky figured it wouldn't have taken long before Edgar decided she *was* the one for him and turned her. Now he was probably pissed off that he hadn't done so already.

When they left the bedroom with the boxes and suitcases, Edgar asked Mandy, "Where are you going?"

Ricky didn't like that he was asking, like he wanted to know just where she was going to be so he could continue to pursue her. Maybe even more so now that she was a cougar too.

"I've got a job. It wouldn't have worked out between us." Mandy continued to head to the door with her suitcases.

Again, Ricky noted she hadn't told him *where* she was moving to.

"I would have turned you if I'd known you would have been fine with it."

She rounded on him, her eyes narrowed in irritation. "I'm *not* fine with it. It was an accident though. If you had turned me on purpose, I would have hated you for it." She walked outside with her suitcases while Hal and Ricky carried out the boxes full of her personal items.

Ricky worried she wasn't fine with him turning her accidentally either.

Once they secured all the stuff in the moving van, they returned to the house to pack her kitchen wares. "You can have all the food. I don't need it," she said to Edgar, who had followed her into the kitchen as if to supervise what she was taking.

"You're moving in with the gimpy guy?" Edgar asked, his tone sarcastic.

"If it's any of your business, I'm moving in with the deputy sheriff and his family."

Ricky wished she had said she was with him, but she was smart to try not to antagonize Edgar too much, when his brothers were watching and listening to everything that was going on. They were careful not to butt in, however.

Edgar watched her as Hal and Ricky helped her box up her kitchen items. Not once did she smile at Ricky or indicate in any way that she had been friends with him long before Edgar had come along. Was she worried about how Edgar would react if he knew Ricky was her old boyfriend? Worse, that he had bitten her? It sure sounded to Ricky like Edgar had planned to turn her eventually, but he'd just been working up to it.

"You didn't tell me you were leaving." Edgar folded his arms and looked cross at her.

"I told you I had to get a job as soon as I had my schooling done."

"Not that you were leaving me."

"I also had told you that it wasn't working out between us. You wouldn't listen to me. Now I have the job in Loveland. So I'm moving there. I have to. I want to. We had some fun times, but now it's time for both of us to move on. It's over between us."

"How come a bunch of deputy sheriffs from Loveland came here with you? Did you tell them you'd have trouble with me when you tried to leave here?" Edgar was surly now.

"No, like I said, I'm staying with the one deputy sheriff and his family. I can't drive now, not since I've been so newly turned."

"How the hell do you think you can work a job since you've just been turned?" Edgar suddenly asked.

Ricky hadn't expected him to ask about that.

"The clinic is cougar run." She motioned to the filled-up boxes. "That's all I want from here. I just need to get some things out of the bathroom and then we can go." She hurried off with a box to pack her stuff in the bathroom while Chase watched the men and Ricky and Hal headed outside with the kitchen stuff.

When Ricky and Hal returned to the house, he expected her to be ready to leave. She was still in the bathroom. "I'll go help her," Ricky said, and hurried off for the bathroom. What he hadn't expected was to see her clothes on the floor, a box packed, and her pacing across the floor as a cougar, her tail whipping about. She lowered her ears when she saw him and growled.

"We're leaving. I'll grab your clothes and the box of stuff. You can be in the Suburban and safe. Just follow me out. Most likely no one will even notice and then we'll be on our way," Ricky told her.

She growled low again, annoyed.

"I know. I'm sorry. It's a pain in the butt in the beginning. But you've got a whole bunch of us to get you through it. You're just one of us now." He was really glad he'd bitten her instead of Edgar. In Durango, she would have been stuck in the apartment, unless there were more cougar shifters here he didn't know about. And she wouldn't have had any other alternative to mate anyone else but Edgar to keep her safe, Ricky suspected, if Edgar had bitten her. Whereas in Yuma Town, they had a whole town of cougar residents who would help take care of her until she adjusted to all of this. She wouldn't have to be confined to a small apartment.

She followed Ricky out of the bathroom and Hal took the box of toiletries, towels, and her clothes from him. Edgar and his brothers were staring at her as if they really couldn't believe she was now one of them and they hadn't been the ones to turn her and keep her.

Edgar frowned. "What clinic is cougar run?"

Ricky smelled the aggression rolling off Edgar in thick waves. His brothers too. Ricky would have felt smugger about it if he really had known that Mandy would be his girlfriend again.

No one told Edgar where the clinic was.

They headed outside and loaded up in the van and the SUV. No one in the other apartments seemed to notice the cougar climbing into the back seat of the SUV. Ricky wondered what kind of work Edgar did. He set her clothes back there in the back seat with her just in case she shifted back on the return drive to Yuma Town.

Before Ricky climbed into the front passenger seat, he heard Edgar say to his brothers, "I'm getting her back."

"You can't go up against a bunch of cougar deputy sheriffs," one of Edgar's brothers said.

Smart man.

Ricky shut his car door and Chase backed out of the parking space, Hal following him with the van. "Did you hear what Edgar said to his brothers?" Ricky asked Chase.

"Yeah, he doesn't know we live in a cougar-run town and everyone will be watching out for Mandy's welfare. The word will go out about the men. I managed to get some pictures of them while they were busy fuming over the situation, and I'll send them out to everyone in the community, including those in Loveland to give them a heads-up."

"Oh, good." Mandy might have pictures of Edgar, but maybe not of his brothers. Ricky was glad Chase thought of it. "Do you think they'll look for her in Loveland?"

"Yeah. Though I'm watching to make sure they don't follow us." Chase turned down another road.

"Oh, yeah." In Ricky's earlier sleuthing-informant days, he was really good at that. But his head was so wrapped around keeping Mandy safe in her current cougar state—he glanced over the back seat and saw that she was lying down, her eyes closed—he wasn't thinking about what Edgar and his brothers were sure to do.

"Too bad we couldn't have made them believe she was just moving to somewhere else in Durango."

"They'd know we didn't work there, and probably that we didn't have a cougar-run clinic."

"Do you think they even believed that part of the story?" Ricky was hopeful they didn't.

Chase smiled at him. "No. Who would ever think we'd have a whole cougar-run town."

Ricky took a deep breath and let it out. "Yeah. You're right."

"It's a long way to Yuma Town though." Chase got a call on his Bluetooth. "Yeah, Hal, what's up?"

"What do you want to do about these guys following us to Yuma Town?"

"We let them follow us and we'll deal with them, or we try to lose them somewhere. But that will be damn hard to do with you driving that van and while we're traveling together. I don't want us to split up though. I'll call Dan and get back with you on that."

"Okay, because I think there is a red car and a black pickup following us already."

Chase called Dan right away.

"If you're calling, I figure you've got trouble," Dan said.

"Yeah, it turns out that Mandy's boyfriend—"

She lifted her head and growled from the back seat.

"Uh, ex-boyfriend and his two brothers are cougars. It looks like they're following us, so I don't think they were happy that Mandy was turned by one of our own and is coming to live with us."

"That's too damn bad for them."

"Yeah, I agree. So I think the best thing to do is to let them follow us into town, our territory, and give them a welcoming committee. I don't see any way of losing them and I don't think we should go out to Hal's ranch. Not until we can go there without them following us."

"Okay, we'll be ready. Do you think you need some of us to meet you halfway?"

"It wouldn't hurt in case these guys think they're going to stop us. Though I really believe they want to see where we end up. Mandy told them she was moving to Loveland," Chase said.

"Nina and Stryker are on their way to meet up with you. I'll stay here and coordinate things," Dan said.

"Okay, good. Thanks, Dan."

"No problem. Mandy's one of us and we're thrilled to have a new LPN working at the clinic when she can manage."

"I'm going too," Leyton said in the background.

"Leyton Hill is a Cougar Special Forces agent and married to Doc Kate and Stryker Hill's twin brother," Ricky told Mandy.

"Okay, Leyton's on his way also. They should intercept you in about an hour and a half," Dan said.

"All right. Thank them and we'll see them soon." Chase told Hal what was going on.

"Good. I like it when we outnumber the bad guys as much as possible."

6

"I'd join you back there as a cougar if it would make you feel any better," Ricky told Mandy.

"No, you wouldn't," Chase said. "Not with your leg in a walking cast. You'd lose the cast and your leg hasn't had time to set properly yet."

Mandy suddenly shifted and hurried to put on her clothes. "Chase is right. Besides, I don't need you to babysit me as a cougar."

"I just thought you might feel more like one of us." Ricky didn't mean to get on her bad side with the comment. *Women.*

"Well, I don't. This is so annoying. And don't tell me I'll get used to it. I'm sure I will. Given time. But right now? It's irritating!"

Ricky and his brother hadn't really seen it that way. They'd had fun every time the shift came upon them. But they'd been younger, and they'd had each other. Plus, they were guys, so he was sure that had something to do with it.

He would do everything he could, and he knew everyone else would too, to make her feel more comfortable about the issues she was dealing with. He climbed over the console with the greatest difficulty to reach Mandy in the middle seat.

"What are you doing?" she asked, as he tried to move his casted leg and groaned and winced.

"Coming back there to bandage your hand. The first aid kit is back there."

Once he got settled and had his seatbelt on, he started to bandage her hand.

"*You* could be a nurse."

He smiled. "I've always wanted to chase down bad guys ever since I was an informant, helping law enforcement agencies to catch them, but I've had a lot of emergency first-aid training in the event I'm the first one on the scene of an accident or a crime scene." He was trying to be gentle, but she tensed, and he knew he was hurting her. He finally finished bandaging her and hoped she wouldn't turn again for a while. Running around on her injured paw would keep it from healing quickly.

"What does Edgar and his brothers work at?" Ricky asked. They were muscular and tanned and they looked like they did work outside, rather than working at a desk in some office.

"Construction work, all three of them."

That's what he'd figured.

Then they all saw flashing lights ahead on the road and knew more help was on the way.

"That's Stryker and Leyton," Chase said, sounding relieved. He pulled over to the shoulder of the road and the others joined him.

"Dan told us to set up a roadblock," Stryker said to Chase as he got out of the Suburban.

"The car and the pickup that had been following us are back there." Chase motioned behind them to the road. "But they backed off as soon as they saw your flashing lights and now, they've even turned off their headlights. I suspect they're sitting on the side of the road in the dark. Since they're cougars, they know we can see them in the dark, so I imagine they're parked far enough back that we can't see them."

"We'll take it from here. You and Hal head to his ranch and Leyton, Nina, and I will keep a roadblock here," Stryker said. "At first, Dan thought we'd just deal with them in our territory, but he'd rather you get Mandy safely to the ranch first."

"Okay, well, be careful." Chase climbed back into his SUV and he and Hal returned to the road, heading back toward the ranch.

Ricky watched out the sideview mirror, but the pickup truck and car didn't approach. He suspected Edgar and his brothers felt out of their element when Chase called on more deputy sheriffs to join them. Ricky couldn't be gladder to be part of the cougar network of Yuma Town and he couldn't wait to serve as a deputy sheriff too so he could take down the bad guys.

"They won't be able to find me, will they?" Mandy asked.

"While you're at the ranch? Most likely not," Chase said. "Courtesy of our close-knit community. They can ask away, but no one will tell them where you're staying. And then our office will be alerted that the men are making inquiries. That scenario would only happen if they have some idea that you're staying in Yuma Town. As far as what you've told them, they believe you're going to Loveland. They won't find you there if they check all the clinics and hospitals in the area. Did you cancel your interview?"

"Yeah, regrettably, before we ate breakfast. I mean, I don't regret working here, I'm glad for it, particularly since that job wasn't a sure deal. But I just hated canceling on them at such a late date." She smiled. "I did have some satisfaction in telling them I already had a job though."

Chase frowned. "Did you tell them where, if the men

happen to go to that place and they say you got a job elsewhere?"

"I told them Denver. I figured that was big enough that it would be even harder for Edgar and his brothers to locate me. I only told them Loveland in the beginning because I had the interview there and I was afraid Edgar might have learned of it."

"Okay, good. Now, if by chance you begin working at the clinic in Yuma Town, and they're checking all the areas near Loveland for a cougar-run clinic, they might try to see you there, but we'll all be on the lookout for them also. I'm certain after a while, they'll give up on the notion."

Ricky sure hoped so, but he didn't think Edgar looked like the giving up or forgiving kind of guy. He was certain Edgar would love to tear into him cougar to cougar because he had to realize, as much as Mandy wasn't trying to let on that Ricky and she had a former relationship, Edgar would have wondered why he would have come to help her when his leg was in a cast.

"Good. I sure hope they give up because I have no intention of renewing my relationship with Edgar or living in Durango any further. Not that I didn't like living there, but I wanted to make a fresh start."

Ricky was glad for that.

When they finally arrived at the ranch, Chase got a call from Stryker and he put it on speakerphone as they began to unload the SUV and van.

Tracey came out with the kids and they were all chattering about making spaghetti for lunch.

The girls grabbed Mandy's hands and wanted to show her the ghosts they'd made to hang in the trees. A purple, a lime green, an orange one, and one white one.

Ricky smiled at her. Mandy glanced at him as if she thought he might rescue her. The boys ran along side of her, telling her they'd made the orange and white one.

He helped take her suitcases into the house, while Hal and Chase started bringing in the boxes of stuff. Tracey directed them to take her kitchen supplies into a storage room and anything else Mandy wanted stored there. Kolby and Ted were soon helping and then Tracey directed everyone to the dining room to have dinner.

Ricky made sure Mandy sat next to him at the table instead of Kolby, which amused the two of them.

"Man, does this bring back memories," Kolby teased him. "As soon as he met Mandy, he was totally wrapped up in her and forgot all about me."

"She might need help with her food," Ricky said, frowning at his brother. He didn't need his brother giving him grief over trying to get back together with Mandy.

She only smiled and sat next to him.

He helped her with cutting up her spaghetti, the way she wanted to eat it.

Stryker called Chase, and he put the call on speakerphone. "Yeah, what's going on with these guys?" Chase asked.

"We went after them, but they took off and went back to Durango, we figure."

"Okay, then they have no idea where Mandy went."

"No. But we're on alert."

"Thanks, Stryker."

Then they ended the call, and Chase patted Mandy's good hand. "We'll keep you safe and here."

"Thank you. All of you," Mandy said, wiping away tears.

Ricky was undone. He reached over and put his hand on her arm and lightly squeezed.

"I'm sorry. I just never thought I'd be in such a weird predicament, that I'd be a furry creature sometimes against my will, that you all are cougars, and so are Edgar and his brothers. I worry about working and not working. Of being a burden."

"Don't," Tracey said, passing the garlic bread around the table. "If any newly turned shifters were a problem, it was the wild Jones boys, but they were endearing and Ted gained himself a couple of sons, like Hal and I did."

Ted laughed. "Yeah, they would shift while they were supposed to be cleaning out the stables and race across the meadows and into the woods playing. They had a blast. It was just a way of dealing with the change. That's one really nice thing about the ranch. We have acres of land for you to run freely on, though I'd take someone with you so you don't get lost. You can probably use your sense of smell to make it back okay, but we don't want to risk it. And I'm way too young to be a dad to these two. Older brother, yeah."

"I'm sure someone will go with me," she said, glancing at Ricky.

And that made him smile.

MANDY DIDN'T KNOW why she had been so upset at the meal. She guessed she was finally coming to the realization her life was truly forever altered and it would never be the same. She was trying to come to grips with it, pretending she could deal with this, but it all just sort of hit her at once.

"You'll get through this." Tracey was such an optimistic bright spot, her words cheered Mandy and she knew she would too.

But she figured she'd have ups and downs about this no matter how much everyone encouraged her that she would be just fine in time.

"Have you told Mandy about the fun Halloween party we're having?" Tracey asked.

"Yeah, Ricky told me. I've got a Steampunk costume."

"Me, too," Ricky said.

Kolby shrugged. "I haven't dressed in a steampunk outfit for eons. I will too."

"I'm going as a cowboy," Ted said, winking. "Well, Wyatt Earp."

They all laughed.

"My daughters, Zoey and Sadie are going as steampunk fairies," Chase said.

"Aww, how cute." Mandy thought this could be the best fun, if she didn't turn during the party and ruin it for herself.

"I wish I could run with you now or as soon as you have to shift," Ricky said.

"You need to heal first. And really, my hand needs to heal also. It's better, but running for a long time in the woods as a cougar would hurt."

Tracey had taken the kids to the family room to watch an animated movie while Kolby and Hal cleaned the dishes.

"I usually help with the dishes, but I think they want to give me a break," Ricky said. "I need to elevate my foot. Do you want to go outside and sit out by the firepit?"

"Yeah, sure, I'd love to. And then I'm going to bed early. It's been a long day with being up so long last night too."

"Me too."

Chase headed home to his family, telling Mandy he was glad she was part of their cougar family. Hal started a fire in the firepit for Mandy and Ricky as they pulled on their jackets to go outside. "I'm off to help read bedtime stories and put the kiddoes to bed."

"Thanks, Hal," they both said to him.

It was really nice being out here like this and she had to admit she enjoyed being with Ricky again. Hal had moved a footstool over so Ricky could prop up his leg, and she sat next to him cuddling. He sighed, their breaths frosty in the chilly air.

Tracey came out and gave them blankets and hot cocoa. "Hal and I are watching something on TV. The kids are in bed. Kolby and Ted are going to the bunkhouse to watch something. If you need anything, just holler. Hal will put out the fire when you want to go to bed."

"Thanks," both Mandy and Ricky said.

When she left, Ricky said, "Are you really all right about everything? About having to live here with us and the business with the shifting?"

"About living here with all of you, I think this is a great friendly place to be. About the shifting business? That's going to take time to get used to."

"I'm serious about helping you through this. I can't wait to run with you on the ranch as soon as I can shift."

She drank her hot cocoa and snuggled against Ricky again, staring up at the stars. "Do you think this was meant to be?"

"Us finding each other again?"

"Me running you over?"

He chuckled. "I hope you're not too glad about that."

She smiled. "When you first left, yeah, I would have felt justified. We were going to a Halloween party, you know. And you just up and disappeared."

"I was helping to take down real boogeymen. I didn't have a choice. Tracey was in trouble. I had to save her." Then he leaned down and kissed Mandy, the sweet cocoa and whipped cream he'd had flavoring his lips and tongue.

This was the Ricky she knew. Fun-loving, adventuresome, at times reckless, and loyal, until he left without word. She'd thought he'd died! But then she'd seen his brother in the grocery store and he had only told her Ricky was doing some work and had to be out of town.

Taking down bad guys? Getting bitten by a cougar shifter? Moving to Yuma Town? She'd thought he was still in Durango, but he was avoiding her and the usual places he took her, like the movies or the mall, or their favorite taco and burger places. In her wildest imagination, she would never have suspected any of this.

But this felt right, kissing him again, snuggling by a fire like when they went camping together. "You said you wanted to be an FBI agent when you were old enough. I thought you were all talk."

He sighed. "I knew I was going to be an informant, that I had information that could put some bad guys behind bars. I hadn't done anything wrong, nothing illegal, so I was a good witness. But I suspected it wouldn't land me a job in the FBI or a sheriff's department. Though I'd always wanted to be a lawman."

"Dan put you through all the training, didn't he?" she asked.

"Yeah. All the law enforcement types did from the sheriff's department to the FBI, CIA, and other special agents with different agencies. They've been like real family. Like the family we haven't had for years. We've gotten in trouble for causing mischief sometimes, but they love us still."

She smiled, then sighed. "I've got to go to bed. I need to unpack my clothes tomorrow, but for tonight, I'm exhausted. No more getting up in the middle of the night to growl at you."

He laughed. "My door is always open to you if you want to drop by and visit."

She took the blankets and helped him up, then he grabbed their empty cocoa mugs and they went inside, him hobbling after her.

"I'll put out the fire," Hal said, "and I'll call Kolby to tell him he needs to escort you back to the bunkhouse to make sure you don't fall on the way over there, Ricky."

"I'll be all right," Ricky said, sounding like he wanted to be a tough deputy sheriff, not coddled by everyone.

"Good night, Ricky." Mandy wrapped her arms around his neck and gave him a deeper kiss, his hands around her waist, pulling her close while Hal went outside to put out the fire in the pit.

"Night, Mandy. I know this isn't what you wanted, but I, for one, am glad you're back in my life."

She gave him a "be careful" look and he smiled.

"Even if it doesn't mean we'll be more than friends," he said.

But she was certain he wanted more than that. "Right. Friends." She wasn't sure what she wanted. She usually was a lot surer of herself, but this whole cougar business had her rattled.

She wondered what she'd do when she finally started working at the clinic. Get a place of her own in town? Then worry about shifting at the wrong time and want to run? She guessed there was time enough to consider what she would do later.

Her cell phone suddenly jingled. Pulling it out of her pocket, she saw the caller was Edgar.

Great. She was ready to go to sleep, hoping she wouldn't shift during the night and take a walk on the wild side again, and think of only the nice night she'd had with the Haverton family and with Chase and Ricky, his brother, and Ted.

"Yeah, Edgar?"

"You know the gimpy guy you were with earlier today? I remember him now. You were dating him, and he dumped you. It was right before Halloween. You mentioned him because you wanted to go to a Halloween party this year after not having gone to one since you broke up with him."

"And you said you don't dress up for silly stuff like that any longer. So you weren't going yourself anyway."

"So you took up with the bastard again? Just to go with

someone to a Halloween party? You'll never make it through the night without shifting. Hell, he doesn't deserve you. And he hasn't heard the last of me." Edgar hung up her.

"What did he want?" Ricky asked, frowning.

"He intends to cause trouble." And she really didn't want him to cause any trouble for Ricky.

7

Ricky hated that Mandy had an ex-boyfriend who intended to continue to bother her. Why couldn't Edgar just man-up and realize she wasn't the one for him any longer? Ricky didn't want her getting hurt. He just wished he could get out of this cast so he could be better prepared in the event the guy showed up in Yuma Town. He suspected Edgar would come after Ricky before he was completely healed.

The air was crisp and chilly as he hobbled back to the bunkhouse with Kolby. "I'm sorry Hal called you to come escort me back to the house. I could have managed on my own." Ricky was glad Mandy had kissed him like she wanted to get back together with him. All the years that had passed between them seemed a distant memory.

"Nah, don't worry about it. You would have done the same for me." Kolby glanced at him. "So what do you think? Are the two of you getting back together again?"

"I hope so, but she and I aren't the same two people as we were before." Even though he felt like she was the same girl he knew, deep down, he knew they weren't. "We've had different life experiences, we're older, and she's got a lot to deal with being a cougar now."

"So you're getting together again." Kolby smiled at him.

Ricky groaned. "I wish. But Edgar called her, and he's got it in for me. What if she goes back to him because she's afraid for my safety?"

"She's got everything going for her here. A whole cougar town to help her through this and to be her family, a job like she's wanted, and you. So no, I don't see her giving that up just to protect you. She was planning to leave him before she was bitten, wasn't she?"

"Yeah."

"Well, see?"

Ricky still worried she might be too concerned about his welfare. He didn't want her to be. He just wanted her to be happy.

"Did you call Dan to let him know the trouble that could be headed your way?"

"Not yet."

"He's your boss. So you'd better get on it."

"I will."

When they reached the bunkhouse, the former main ranch house before the Haverton family built the new one, Ricky said goodnight to his brother. Ted already had retired to his own bedroom in the rustic house that was designed for cowboys or guests of the Havertons with four bedrooms, four baths, honey-oak wood floors, walls, and ceilings, and paintings of the horses they'd raised on the ranch over the years. It also had a spacious living room for kicking back after long days working on the ranch and a kitchen they all cooked in when they weren't sharing meals with the Havertons.

He hadn't given it much thought about living closer to work when he was going to be on the road quite a bit in his deputy sheriff job. He still planned to help out at the ranch on his days off, but he wondered if Hal and Tracey would want to replace him with another hired hand who would work more hours than he would be able to. There was still a spare bedroom, but they might need his room if he wasn't going to be a full-time ranch hand. No one had said a thing about it, and he hadn't started working as a full-time deputy yet, so he figured they'd all just play it by ear.

Each of the rooms had their own private door that led outside the bunkhouse, which made it nice if they were all working different hours, which sometimes they did. And each of the doors had their own cat door that they could slip out of any time they felt the urge to run, which, when Ricky and Kolby had first been turned, had come in really handy. One or the other of them would run through the other brother's cat door, snarl to wake the other up, and then the brother would shift, and they'd slip off into the night, running through the wild to their heart's content. On occasion, they'd miscalculate the timing of the shift, back in those days, and one of them would end up walking back to the house naked. Not the best thing to do when it was cold and having to walk on rocks and the prickly ground. The one who was still a cat would race back to the house and wake a perturbed Ted up to come to the brother's rescue.

Getting ready for bed, Ricky smiled as he remembered Ted riding out, trailing another horse behind and having a set of clothes for the brother who had shifted inconveniently. He grumbled a lot about times like that, but they knew he loved working with them too. And spending quality time talking about everything under the sun, riding the horses, and relaxing after a hard day's work. Both Ricky and Kolby owed so much to Ted for mentoring them, and acting as a father figure, though he constantly told them he was not old enough to be their father, which made them all the more determined to tell him he was better than any father they could have had.

"Brother, older brother, fine. Not your father." Ted was still trying to find his own mate, so he really didn't want a prospective mate thinking he'd had two kids when he'd been a teen.

Ricky swung his casted leg into bed, then picked up his cell phone and called Dan. "Hey, I hope it's not too late to be calling you, but Edgar, Mandy's ex-boyfriend, called her and said he isn't letting things stand as they are now. So I expect trouble, and probably before I'm all healed up."

"Okay, no, you know it's never too late to call me when trouble could be headed our way. Get some sleep. I'll let everyone else know."

"Thanks." Then Ricky nestled back against his pillows and pulled the down comforter over his waist and thought about Mandy and the kiss they had shared. Passionate, real, loving. He was determined to make her his, whatever it took.

IN THE MIDDLE of the night, Mandy found herself waking to that familiar feeling she had now that she was going to shift. She wanted to snarl and bite Ricky! She needed her eight hours of sleep to feel human. This was not helping one bit.

At least she'd left her door ajar so she could leave the room. She yanked off her pajamas and then pulled off the bandages on her hand that Ricky had so carefully wrapped around her injury. She stared at her hand for a moment, couldn't believe it, and smiled. It was much better. Much better than if she'd been strictly a human. Then the annoyance returned as her body heated right before the shift into her cougar form that she couldn't stop for anything.

She tried to tell herself he hadn't bitten her hand on purpose. It didn't matter. She was totally frustrated. She went into the bathroom and looked at herself in the full-length mirror, the first time she'd actually seen herself as a cougar. No matter how many times she tried to reconcile with herself that that was really *her* with the pretty reddish fur and black tipped ears, the white fur under her chin and on her belly, she couldn't.

She ran out of the bathroom and through the hall to the front door that had a cat door for them to come and go as cougars. Luckily, she was able to get out that way without alerting anyone else in the family. She didn't want to wake up the whole household while she was having a cat fit over being a cougar when she wanted to sleep, and they needed their sleep just as much!

Once she was outside, she felt better, like she blended in with the wild out of doors, that she was meant to be there. Was that ridiculous, or what?

Then the annoyance returned, and she ran straight for the bunkhouse. Normally, she could curb her irritation when something bothered her, no problem. Was it the cougar half of her that made her so snarly feeling?

She wandered around the dark bunkhouse, a couple of lights on outside the house and the main house and the barn, though with her cat vision, she realized how much she loved being able to see just as well as if it were daylight out.

She smelled the doors to the house, surprised there were so many of them leading to the outside of the place. One smelled more like Ricky's scent than the others and she pushed through the cat door within the door.

Inside the room was dark, though she could see just fine.

Ricky had a double bed, a blue, down comforter covering

him, his eyes closed in sleep, like hers should have been. She sat her rump on the blue and brown and beige braided, oval rug for a few minutes, glowering at him. Of course, he didn't wake, too busy sleeping happily, and that annoyed her further.

She jumped on his lap liked she'd done when he was in the clinic and glowered at him. Though she wasn't sure if her human attempt at a cougar glower had the same effect.

His eyes popped open, and for a moment, he just stared at her. Then he smiled.

That was *not* the response she was hoping for. Being sorry for the condition she was in? Maybe. An apology? Sure. Smiling? No way.

She growled.

He chuckled. "Sorry."

He didn't mean it in the least!

"If I could, I'd shift and go running with you. But I might rebreak my leg and Doc Kate would be furious with me. And I want this cast off when I take you to the Halloween party."

She frowned.

"Listen, I was thinking of getting a home on Secret Valley Creek Road. For us. It has woods, a creek, and my boss, Dan, and his mate, Addie, also a deputy sheriff, and their twin babies, live there. So does Florence Fitzgerald. She's a retired CIA officer. Now she owns a bakery in town and they're the best sweet treats ever. I want to take you there. Tomorrow maybe? If you think you can manage the shifting a little? Mrs. Fitz had a news reporter, newly turned, working as her baker and he would just duck back into the office off the kitchen when he had to shift until it was safe to come out. I had to go out the kitchen door one time myself, so it's a viable option."

She looked skeptically at him. She couldn't even begin to believe he thought they should get a house together.

He patted the bed beside him. "Sleep with me. You can wear

some of my clothes when you wake, and I'll walk you back to the main house."

As wired as she'd been when she first had shifted, she felt exhausted now, and she agreed. Though she didn't have plans to wake him when she needed to walk back to the main house. She'd make her way back to the house on her own.

He pulled the cover aside so she could climb under it with him and she suspected he worried she'd turn and then be sleeping naked on top of the covers and would get cold. He pulled her closer so she could rest her head against his T-shirt covered chest. She was going to resist, but the fight was all out of her and she laid her head down on his chest, listening to his heart beating, the blood rushing through his veins. She was thinking she would wake if she shifted into her human form and she would grab some of his clothes, not wake him, and leave. No way did she want him to have to hobble back to the main house and to the bunkhouse again in his cast.

Then she drifted off and finally woke to the sound of Kolby knocking on the door. Her heart hammered. *Great. Just great.*

"Hey, Ricky, are you awake? Mandy's missing. We're hoping she's running as a cougar and okay, but we're getting ready to search for her. We figured you could ride your horse."

Ricky smiled at her and Mandy groaned and pulled the covers over her head.

"Call off the search. She's here with me."

"Oh, great, that's a relief. So, does that mean we have to have a shotgun wedding?"

Ricky threw his pillow at the door with a thump.

Kolby laughed. "Hey, Ted, she's been found. We need to call off the search. She's safe and under Ricky's protection."

"I need to get out of here," she told Ricky, not believing she was naked in bed with him, though *he* was wearing a T-shirt and boxer shorts and a clunky cast. She was glad for that anyway.

She couldn't believe that she'd fallen so deeply asleep that she hadn't realized she was snuggling with him in her human form at some point in the middle of the night, when, in the beginning, she'd wanted to bite him. He didn't know how lucky he had been.

8

R icky couldn't believe they'd slept so soundly that he hadn't even awakened when Mandy had shifted. The two of them had both had to deal with the trauma of his bite to her hand and his broken leg and minor concussion and moving from his room to hers and her doing the same with coming to his room at the clinic that night, which had to be the reason why they were so exhausted last night.

He could have socked his brother for making the shotgun-wedding comment though. Ricky knew Mandy was feeling self-conscious about sleeping naked against him during the night when they were just getting to know each other again, especially since everyone in the family would know about it by breakfast time.

"Wait here. I'll get you some clothes." He climbed out of bed and pulled some blue sweats out of his bottom bureau drawer and handed them to her. "They might be a little big. We'll get some shoes for you. I'm going to the bathroom so you can get dressed."

He left her alone and was thinking how he would be all for a shotgun wedding, really.

When he returned to the bedroom, she was dressed in his sweats and he wanted to wrap his arms around her, but she hurried past him to the bathroom.

"We could get married," Ricky said, getting dressed.

"Ha!" She left the bathroom and she tied her hair in a ponytail. "You might not feel that way if you knew what I wanted to do when I came to see you last night."

He smiled. As growly as she'd looked, he'd known. "Bite me."

"Yeah."

"But you love me."

"Don't push your luck."

Kolby knocked at the door. "Hey, Ted and I made pumpkin spice pancakes and slices of ham for you guys. We're headed out to take care of the horses. Tracey dropped by to bring some of Mandy's clothes over for her."

"Hey, brother, thanks so much." Ricky left the bedroom and got the clothes for Mandy and left them in the room for her. "See you in a few minutes," he said to her.

He walked out of the room and thanked his brother and Ted too before they headed outside.

"I hope you plan to marry that little filly," Ted said, putting on his Stetson.

"I'm working on it." Though Ricky was sure it was going to take some time to make things right between them. Maybe when she had her shifting under control, though that could take months, she would consider such a thing. He just couldn't wait to be able to run with her as a cougar, to cuddle with her as one too, when she had to turn at night and couldn't help herself, to show her that it was just a natural thing for them to do.

Then Kolby and Ted left the bunkhouse and Mandy joined Ricky in the kitchen and smiled when she saw that the pancakes were wearing powdered sugar and maple syrup, forming jack-olantern smiles. Her mood brightened in an instant. She usually had a sunny disposition, so it was disconcerting for him to see her down about any of this and he was glad she was cheered up.

Ricky brought them cups of coffee and sat down at the table with Mandy, who had changed into her own clothes—a soft, rust-colored sweater and blue jeans and boots. He was thinking he ought to get her some western ones so she could ride a horse in style. "Ted and Kolby are great, aren't they?"

"This is really cute." She ate some of the pancakes. "And they're delicious."

"We all love to cook. Ted was the one who taught us." Ricky sighed. "You know, they're expecting me to make things right between us, so I think there's a bit of matchmaking going on here."

She shook her head, but then she got a call from Edgar and she groaned. She put it on speakerphone so Ricky could listen in and he appreciated it.

"You're not working in Loveland. I checked all the clinics, but I found one that said you got a job in Denver. Don't worry. I'll find you." Then Edgar hung up on her.

Ricky would recognize Edgar's gruff voice anywhere. He hated that she'd gotten involved with him in the first place, wishing Ricky could have stayed with her instead and fended off the likes of Edgar. How could the guy think she'd want to return to him after all his bullying? "Are you going to change your cell number?"

"Yeah, I am."

"Why don't you move in with me? I mean, us?" Ricky asked. "We have another spare bedroom with its own bathroom. Then if you shift in the middle of the night and you want to bite me, you can join me in the bedroom. I'll leave the door ajar for you. I mean, I thought you might want some female companionship initially to learn all there is about us, like from Tracey and Leesa, the children's nanny, but I'd love to have you here, close by." She opened her mouth to say no, he was certain. "That way if you aren't at the main house because you've shifted and taken off, no one will worry about sending out a search party. Besides, it's much quieter at the bunkhouse than it is there with all the three-year-olds playing."

She seemed to reconsider and sighed. "You might be right. But I need to get a place of my own once I can start working and control the shifting."

Yes! "Okay, great. I'll help you move your things over."

"I'll call Tracey and see if it's okay first."

He figured she didn't want to rock the boat when Hal and Tracey had been so generous in letting her stay with them. But he knew they'd understand and if she was going to constantly come to see him in the middle of the night, they'd feel less anxious about her disappearing from the main house.

She got on her phone and called Tracey when he got a call and he started clearing away the dishes. It was from Dan and Ricky told him about the situation with Mandy and Edgar now searching for her in Denver.

"Good. It will take Edgar a while to do that. I was planning to have you work in the office until Doc removes your cast, but I want you on a special detail," Dan said.

"Yes, sir?"

"You'll be in protective services for Ms. Richards. I want you to stick with her until we're assured she's going to be safe from Edgar and his brothers."

"Okay, that sounds good to me. She's asking Tracey right now if she can move to the bunkhouse and use the spare bedroom."

Mandy nodded at him.

"Tracey said it's a go," Ricky told Dan.

"Hal's getting Ted and Kolby to help get me moved over here.

Hal said you're to stay here and wait for me, not to stumble around on your walking cast again. I'll be back in a few minutes," Mandy said.

"Dan put me on protective service duty to watch out for you."

Dan said, "You can wait at the house until she gets moved over. The other guys will watch out for her in the meantime."

"I want to take her to Fitz's Bakery and Coffee Shop for a treat." Ricky didn't want to wait to begin taking Mandy to special places on dates to prove to her how much she really meant to him and how much he enjoyed being with her.

"Wait until she's got her shifting more under control. You don't want to stress her out. You'll both enjoy it more then. Hal said she took off last night as a cougar and joined you," Dan said.

"She did." Ricky let his breath out on a sigh, resigned to do this Dan's way. "All right. Maybe I'll take her riding."

"With your leg in a cast? Why don't you just watch TV together. I've got to go. Thanks for the heads-up on these guys. Keep me posted if anything else comes up."

"Will do."

When they ended the call, Mandy said, "I don't know the first thing about riding horses. And you shouldn't be trying to ride a horse while wearing a bulky cast. Poor horse."

"All right. Well, you tell me what you want to do, and I'll make it happen."

MANDY WAS SO glad that she was moving to the bunkhouse, mostly because she knew she'd continue to return there if she shifted at night. And she wanted to date Ricky again. She hoped they'd have some time alone to watch TV and just visit with each other without Kolby and Ted being around, but she didn't want them to feel like they had to leave the bunkhouse to give them privacy either. It was their home and they worked hard during the day and deserved a place to relax at night.

But it all worked out in the end, everyone doing everything they could to give Ricky and Mandy the chance to be together as a couple for three whole weeks. She'd changed her cell phone number and she hadn't had any more issues with Edgar. She'd even managed to start working as a nurse at the clinic. Rick's cast had been removed, and his leg was all healed up. For the first time, he went out on patrol as a deputy sheriff today.

That evening, many of the cougars in town would celebrate her and Ricky's birthdays. She'd never expected anything like that would happen. She'd gotten Ricky a new Stetson and cowboy boots so he could wear them on the job and off. She hoped he liked them.

They both returned to the Haverton's ranch to a barbecue, a big chocolate cake with a cowboy and a nurse and two cougars sitting on top, ice cream, and hayrides to commemorate the day Mandy and Ricky were both born in Cody, Wyoming only fifteen minutes apart on October tenth at the same hospital, by the same doctor, twenty-one years ago. To meet each other when they were in high school, to learn they were born in the same small town, in the same hospital, and on the same day had cemented their relationship way back then. She didn't think they'd ever be celebrating their birthdays together again after they'd broken up and that made this birthday even more special for the both of them.

She couldn't believe it when he gave her a cowgirl hat and cowgirl boots so she could ride horses with him in style. She hugged and kissed him, and he was just as happy to get her presents for his birthday. After the festivities, they had to shift and run as cougars, the first time since Ricky's cast had come off.

He'd been dying to run with her as a cougar and she was thrilled that he finally could.

Everyone who had attended the party went running as cougars, and she loved it, loved being with Ricky in this special way. She ran beside him as if they were together for real, still not really used to being with other cougars in a social way, but she was quickly learning how wonderful it was to share her experiences as a big cat with others.

Ricky was being affectionate with her like she saw some of the mated cougars being with one another, brushing up beside her, licking her cheek, nuzzling her face, then racing off again with her in hot pursuit. Then he'd turn on a dime and go after her and she'd whip around and race off. But he was determined to catch her, and she was just as determined to keep out of his reach. It didn't work and he soon tackled her, claws retracted, and took her down. She snarled and gently bit at him, keeping her claws retracted, something she had to learn to do. It was such a natural instinct to extend her claws in a "fight," even if the fight was just for fun. She hadn't realized how much fun she could have with Ricky as a cougar.

Then everyone returned to the ranch house, shifted and dressed, and said goodnight.

"Thanks again for the lovely boots and the hat," she said to Ricky.

"Thanks for mine. Now I can take you horseback riding."

"I'm looking forward to it when we have some time off from work. How was your first day on the job?" She was so glad Edgar hadn't found her in Yuma Town for the last three weeks. She hoped that he had given up on her. But she was thrilled that Ricky was a deputy sheriff too, and he could really protect her if she needed him to.

"I just gave some people passing through the area citations

for speeding, helped a cat out of a tree, nothing really wild. What about you with your nursing duties?"

"It was pretty quiet. I helped Doc William with casting a broken leg. That was my first time. I'm so glad I got to help remove your cast."

"I felt I was in the best of hands."

She smiled. "I feel that way with you watching over me."

Everyone had returned home, and Ricky and Mandy sat on the back patio of the bunkhouse and started up the firepit, then roasted marshmallows, cuddling with each other on a couple's swing, and enjoying the stars on the black night. Their marshmallows melty and devoured, they licked each other's mouths and kissed and tongued each other, enjoying the sweet taste.

"You know we're going to have to mate," Ricky said, groaning as they kissed with heated abandon. He really wanted to take her to bed with him as his mate, but she was still reluctant.

She smiled. "You think you're ready for me?"

"Yeah. I definitely am. I've loved you from the beginning."

She scoffed. "That's why you left me."

"Yeah, the ultimate act of love and sacrifice to protect you. I'm just waiting for you to say you're ready to love me too," Ricky said.

She let out her breath in the frosty night air. "You just want me to come to your bed."

He smiled. "Yeah, I do. For every day and night. Not just because you've shifted and want my company. But for always. To be my mate."

"We've only been back together for three weeks."

"Yeah, and it's my birthday wish."

She laughed and kissed his nose. "I...I want to have more control over my shifting first. Don't give up on me yet. We both have to get up early in the morning for work." She didn't want to tell him that she didn't want to feel like he had to take care of her always because he'd bitten her, and he felt it was his responsibility. She wanted him to marry her as his equal. But there was time enough for that later. When she could control her cougar better.

He sighed. "Okay, I'll ask you again soon though. I'm not giving up that easily."

She smiled and he put out the fire, and then they headed back into the bunkhouse. She knew she wouldn't have to wait long for him to ask again. And he knew she'd be back in his bed as a cougar again tonight. She didn't know why, but she kept shifting mostly at night. During the day she was having more control over it, like she got it out of her system at night. Which was a good thing since she was working now.

She loved working too. Luckily, she'd only had to hide in Doc Kate's office once when she had to unexpectedly shift her first day of work.

After she said goodnight to Ricky, she took her shower and went to bed. She no longer bothered to put on pajamas because invariably in the middle of the night, she'd shift and go to Ricky's room.

That night, she shifted, headed down the hall and into his room, then leapt into his bed. He had been waiting for the moment, pulled his covers aside as usual, but this time? He pulled off his T-shirt and boxers and shifted into his cougar as if this was the most natural way for a couple to sleep. It was the first time he could join her as a cougar after having had his walking cast removed.

This was beginning to be a habit she really didn't want to give up. He hadn't asked her if she wanted to mate again, but if he didn't ask her soon, she was going to suggest it! Maybe at the Halloween party.

She smiled as a cougar. Yeah, three weeks from today, that's just what she'd do.

9

It was finally the day of the Halloween party and Mandy was excited about it! She was working at the clinic and Ricky was doing his deputy sheriffing duty for the day and then they'd return to the bunkhouse and change into their costumes. They'd both helped to decorate the community center last night and she couldn't wait to enjoy the camaraderie of the cougar-organized event.

She'd learned that they didn't wear jewelry because of shifting and the worry of losing it, so she knew Ricky wouldn't be giving her an engagement ring to declare his intentions to marry her. She didn't care. Tonight, with the full moon hanging in the sky, she was proposing to Ricky at the Halloween party, steampunk style. She couldn't wait.

But twice, she'd had to help deliver human babies for women who were just supposed to be passing through Yuma Town and suddenly went into labor.

Dr. Kate said to Mandy, "It's a full moon. I swear it always happens this way."

Elsie was helping Dr. William with a third delivery. It reminded Mandy about how her mother and Ricky's had babies nearly at the same time, only they'd had just the one doctor to deliver them both.

Elsie had come in to help out even on her day off. Marcus was in there helping Elsie too. And then Mandy was responsible for getting the mother settled in her room with the baby while Dr. Kate had to take care of another emergency, an older man with chest pains, a human also passing through the area on his way to Loveland.

When Mandy left the room to see what else she could help with, she saw Edgar in the waiting area and she nearly had a heart attack. He grabbed her, poking a gun in her ribs, his blue eyes cold with hate. "You make a sound and I kill everyone in here. You aren't going to be anybody else's mate."

She knew not to go with him. She knew it. But if he killed the doctors, the nurses, the mothers and their babies, the other patient who came in with the chest pains, she would never be able to live with herself. All she could hope for was that someone would see her being forced into Edgar's car. Outside the clinic, he'd quickly taped her wrists and mouth and shoved her into the trunk of his car.

"You didn't think I'd find you, did you? It took me six weeks, and this was the only clinic in the last town I hadn't searched that was only an hour from Loveland. Here I thought I'd have to make all kinds of inquiries, but I saw your car and smelled your scent, walked inside the clinic, and there you were. Just waiting for me. It's providence, don't you think?" He slammed the trunk closed.

She was alive, and angry, and she wasn't going to let him have his way. What did he think he was going to do with her? Force her to mate him? She suspected he intended to kill her for leaving him.

He'd made the mistake of taping her hands in front of her and she was able to pull the tape off her mouth. And then she pulled the tape off around her wrists and her ankles. She spied the trunk release, but she didn't want to pop the trunk and have him pull the car over and shoot her or knock her out so she couldn't do it again. And she didn't want him having a wreck if he suddenly saw the trunk pop open, and she was injured or killed outright.

She found a crowbar in his car and thought she'd use it on him. But he had a gun and she might not be able to get the advantage. As a cougar, she could leap at him and bite him, and he wouldn't be able to react fast enough. Not as fast as she could move as a cat.

Now, if only she could shift. So far, she couldn't, though she was taking her clothes off in preparation. It would take him some hours to get her to Durango though, if that was where he was taking her, unless he planned to dump her body somewhere closer by.

She didn't want to shift too soon and not be able to hold her cougar form, though she was getting better at this. Then she heard a car's siren, and since she'd learned the difference between each of the sheriff department's vehicles, she knew it was Ricky's. She was so afraid Edgar would shoot Ricky and she tried to shift again. This time she was successful.

Suddenly, the car veered sharply to the left and the road was rough, a dirt road, she suspected, and she was bounced all over the trunk. As a cat, she was more agile, more able to protect herself when the car broke through several saplings and made a big splash. Suddenly, she heard other sirens way off in the distance: Dan's car, Chase's, and Stryker's.

But Ricky's was the closest of all. The trunk began filling with water, and she felt the car sinking, her back pressed against the back of the seat, the car tilting engine down first, the sound of bubbles surrounding the car as it plunged into the blackness.

RICKY HAD BEEN busy checking out a case of a stolen car abandoned twenty miles out of Yuma Town. He called in the license plate number and told the dispatcher that the car needed to be towed in when he saw a red car that he thought he recognized, but not from here. It was tearing off down the road, headed in the direction of Durango.

His heart thundering, the first thought he had was it was Edgar's car. Had Edgar discovered Mandy was working at the clinic? He immediately called her cell phone. If she was with a patient, the call would go to voice mail, which it did. Trying not to panic, he got into his car and headed after the red car. If nothing else, he could get the driver for speeding and confirm who he was to ensure he was or wasn't Edgar.

He called April Hightower, the clinic's receptionist. "Hey, I think I'm following Edgar Sanderson's car heading toward Durango. I just wanted to make sure that Mandy is at work, seeing patients. She's not picking up her phone."

"Hold on, let me check." April got right back on the phone. "She's not here. She's not anywhere."

Ricky's heart nearly seized. "Calling Dan now." He called Dan and said, "I'm in pursuit of what I think is Edgar's car. He's speeding on the highway heading for Durango. I may be wrong, but Mandy's disappeared from the clinic and I'm afraid Edgar's abducted her."

"Hell, I'll get everyone on it. Just keep him in sight."

"You got it." Ricky prayed this was all a big mistake. That Mandy was safe somewhere in town and they'd just misplaced her. That the speeder wasn't Edgar, just someone else breaking the law. But when Ricky called her number again, he only got voicemail and he feared the worse.

Now he was in hot pursuit of the car and close enough to call the tag number in and learned it was Edgar Sanderson's car. The bastard made a sharp turn and tore off on a dirt road near a lake and Ricky quickly made the turn, alerting Dan every step of the way. He could hear the other units' sirens now, but they were still too far away to be of any help.

He prayed that Mandy was still alive. He was finally gaining on the car when Edgar tore off the dirt road into a stand of saplings and plunged the car into the lake. Ricky's heart skipping beats, he told Dan what had happened, stopped the car at the edge of the lake, and raced out to see the car's tail end tipped up, then sinking into the dark water.

"Mandy!" Ricky yanked off his weapons belt and shoes and shirt, then raced into the water until he could dive in and search for the car. Was she still in the car? Was Edgar?

He felt a broken windshield and despite the darkness could see Edgar's lifeless body in the car, but no sign of Mandy. He heard some movement in the trunk. He swam inside the vehicle and maneuvered around Edgar's body to reach the trunk release, but the trunk suddenly popped open before he could do anything.

The next thing he saw was Mandy in her cougar form, peering in through the broken window at him and relieved beyond words, he quickly swam out of the car and touched her face, having to reassure himself she truly was all right. Then the two of them made their way to the surface of the water. He was so grateful she was alive, and he was just as glad Edgar was dead. Since Edgar had been alone, it appeared his brothers hadn't had any involvement in this, which was a good thing for them.

Ricky and Mandy soon reached the shore and he hugged her to his chest. Tears ran down his cheeks, mixing with drops of lake water.

Dan pulled up first, Chase, Stryker and Nina after that. All of them were out of their cars within seconds.

"Edgar was driving the car and he's dead at the wheel. He drowned," Ricky said. And good riddance.

Mandy licked Ricky's cheek and nuzzled her face against his.

"I'm taking her home." And he was asking her to marry him. He intended to tonight at the party, since it was their own special theme and he suspected when they married, they'd make it a steampunk wedding.

Nina brought her a blanket and handed another to Ricky.

"Is she okay? Maybe she needs to be checked out at the clinic," Dan said.

Mandy shook her head and got up and trotted off to Ricky's car, the blanket still covering her back.

"She knows what she wants," Nina said smiling and winked at Dan.

"What about you?" Dan asked Ricky, looking worried.

"I'm good. I nearly had a heart attack, but now that I know Mandy is safe, I'm good." Sopping wet, Ricky grabbed his dry shirt, shoes, and weapons belt off the ground. He headed for the car and opened the back door for Mandy so she could lie down on the back seat. It wouldn't do for anyone to see a cougar sitting in a deputy sheriff's car in the front passenger seat. "Do you mind if I take off the rest of the afternoon?"

"You've got it. We'll see you at the party, won't we?" Dan asked.

Mandy nodded and Ricky smiled. "Nothing will keep us from it."

As soon as they arrived at the bunkhouse, Tracey called to tell them she'd heard what had happened and if they needed anything to let her or Hal know. Kolby and Ted returned from their ranching duties to come and see them too, and Mandy was glad they were so concerned, but she really wanted to chill after all that had happened and just be alone with Ricky.

After hugs and well wishes, Kolby and Ted left, and she headed into the bathroom to shift and shower off the lake water.

"Hey," Ricky said outside the bathroom door that was partially ajar, "I would have died if you had. I want you for my mate for now and always. I love you, Mandy. I was going to declare my love to you at the party tonight, but I want to now."

She opened the bathroom door with her cat's paw, and he smiled at her. "I thought you had shifted already."

She pushed at the glass door with her paw as if urging him to open the door and start the water for her.

He started running the hot water for her. "You can't shift?"

She growled low. She still wanted to take a shower and then get into bed with Ricky, to snuggle with him until she could shift back. She was hoping that she wouldn't shift at the party tonight, since she'd shifted earlier, but then she worried, what if she couldn't shift back at all because she'd been so traumatized?

She growled again and walked into the shower.

"If you promise not to bite me, I'll wash you." He stripped down to his boxer briefs and got into the shower to soap her up. But then she tugged at his boxer briefs and he smiled. "All right." He tossed the wet article of clothing on the tile floor and closed the shower door again. He was beginning to run her vanilla shampoo over her coat when she suddenly shifted.

This was more like it. Her body was covered in soap and she began to rub her soap onto his body. He was quickly aroused, and she was putting the trauma of the last couple of hours out of her mind while she enjoyed touching her mate in the throes of passion, because that's exactly where this was headed. No words were needed now, except maybe, "I love you, Ricky, and always have."

"God, I've wanted to hear you say that forever. I love you,

Mandy, and I couldn't live without you. I mean it."

And then they were soaping each other up again, kissing like they'd never been apart, like it was meant to be, and she knew it was from the moment she'd hit a cougar on the road, he had bitten her, and they had become soulmates, just like in the beginning. Two kids born in the same hospital, practically at the same time, meeting up miles away in a new hometown to become boyfriend and girlfriend, and then meeting here, only this time they were staying together.

He slipped his hand between her legs, started to stroke her, his mouth kissing hers, their tongues tangling, and she was leaning against the tile wall, feeling limp beneath his touch. His free hand ran the soap over a breast, and then the other, her nipples tingling and peaking. His finger stroked her nubbin, eliciting a low moan. She wanted to climb onto him, ride him in the shower under the hot, pulsating spray of water, to feel it sluicing down their bodies, his arousal pressing deep inside her.

The feel of the cold lake water that had chilled her to the core was gone and rampant heat warmed her to the marrow of her bones. Not only from the hot shower, but from the way Ricky was stroking her, bringing her to the brink, making her beg for release. She cried out with elation, the thrumming of the orgasm filling her, and he quickly lifted her, wrapping her legs around his hips, and asked, "Are you sure?"

"Don't ask. Just do it."

He began kissing her again, and plunged his cock into her, slowly, deeply and pulling out and doing it again and again and again. They were Libras—and the two of them brought a sense of balance to their lives in everything they did. She was in heaven with the man of her dreams and she would love him forever.

~

IN HIS WILDEST DREAMS, Ricky had never imagined entering a shower to wash his cougar girlfriend and end up making love to her when she shifted. He'd envisioned making love to her in bed, declaring their love for each other there, mating for life. But this was one hell of a way to go. Especially after the close call they'd had of easily losing each other in the chilly lake water.

Her body fit his just perfectly, tight and accepting, her eyes closed, her lips parted, and he kissed her again, their tongues doing a choreographed dance. He was glad she could put the trauma of the last couple of hours out of her mind to be with him like this, and he still was thanking God for allowing him to come to her rescue, though she had rescued herself in her time of need.

She arched her back and he pressed kisses along her neck and throat and down her breastbone. "Ohmigod," she said, and he felt her climax rippling around his cock.

He thrust again and this time he came, realizing in that moment that he hadn't used a condom. Hell. He hoped if she got pregnant, she would not want to kill him.

They washed off, turned the water off, and toweled each other dry.

"Your bed or mine?" she asked.

"Mine. That's where you always end up."

She smiled. "Yeah. I guess I've always kind of seen it as my bed too. You know, I want a steampunk wedding."

"Sounds great to me." He grabbed her up, wrapped in the towel, and carried her to bed.

"I love your boss."

"Dan? Yeah, he's a great guy."

"How many bosses would give you the rest of the day off to do this?" she asked as Ricky laid her in bed, pulled her towel off, then yanked off his towel and joined her, covering them with the comforter.

"Not any I can think of."

"What if I'm needed at the clinic?" But Mandy didn't make a move to show that she wanted to go back into town. Instead, she curled up against Ricky's body.

"You have a really good boss too. The cougars are always there for each other when we need them the most."

"I never thought it would be like this, living with a cougar community. I was thinking about that home you were talking about that was situated near a creek. I'd like to look at it this weekend when we're both off from work."

Ricky smiled at her. "Sure thing." They were going to get a home of their own. He was finally going to have his own family, along with Kolby, of course. "I have to ask. When I was trying to find the trunk release to rescue you, how did you manage on your own?"

"I knew I couldn't use the trunk release while he was speeding down the road. I could imagine me popping the trunk and him rolling the car. I'd be thrown from the car and killed. I planned to shift and then either pop the trunk when he stopped the car and take him down as a cougar, or just wait until he opened the trunk himself, unaware I had pulled the tape off my wrists and ankles and had shifted into my cougar. I didn't expect him to drive the car into the lake. It took me a few minutes to reach the lever and then yank it hard with my cougar teeth."

"I'm damn glad you did. I was having a hard time reaching the trunk release with his body in the way."

She sighed. "I love you."

"I love you right back, honey."

Mandy was so good for Ricky in so many ways and he couldn't believe how many holidays were coming up that they would celebrate together, making this the most special year ever. And the new year was all theirs.

10

The night of the Halloween party, Ricky couldn't contain his need to tell all of the gathered cougars that he and Mandy were mated. Not only because he wanted them to know they were a couple, but just in case any single male cougar had designs on his girl. But he waited just the same until Mandy was ready to share the news too.

Everyone was dressed in the steampunk theme. The Buchanan's girls had started a trend and all the little girls were steampunk fairies. The boys wore black capes with their jeans, boots, and vests, and Ricky thought they were more like vampires, Batman, or some variation thereof. Most everyone was wearing cowboy boots, and vests, the women in corsets and skirts or striped pants. And Dottie, the former police dispatcher and her husband, Jack, with the Cougar Special Forces, had bought steampunk-goggles for everyone who didn't have a pair. Even Ted wore a pair of the goggles on top of his Stetson.

Mrs. Fitz had made tons of sweets, from a cake decorated with an antique clock to cupcakes decorated with hot air balloons and pumpkin spice bread. And she had joined the fun in wearing a rust leather skirt, jacket, lace blouse, vest, gloves, leather aviator hat, and a cool steampunk pistol.

Bridget and Travis MacKay—who were Cougar Special Forces—had been visiting with her parents in Ely, Minnesota with their twins—and made it just in time for the party, bringing miniature steampunk pocket watches for everyone.

Chase and Shannon had made a pumpkin pie, and Tracey had brought a pecan pie. Docs Kate and William and Kate's mate, Leyton, brought trays of meat, cheeses, fruits, and vegetables.

Deputy Sheriff Nina had come with her mate, Stryker, and her sister, Ava, had come with Kolby, though Ricky still didn't think the two of them were serious about each other.

They had another special occasion to celebrate too, and that was Dan's birthday. Ricky still couldn't believe he was working for him now. Well-wishes and presents were given to their beloved sheriff, his wife, Addie, giving him a big kiss, but then she had to go off and nurse their four-month old twins.

The music was playing in the background—steampunk music that was a mixture of fantasy, world music, and steam mechanics. It had a great beat and several couples and singles were dancing to the music.

Dan got up to the podium to welcome their newest member to the community, Mandy Richards. When she came up to the podium, she dragged her gun-toting mate with her. He smiled at her, loving her.

"Thanks to all of you for helping me to get through the first six weeks of this wild and crazy ride of being a part-time cougar. I want to thank Docs Kate and William for helping me in my new job. And I want to thank everyone for protecting me when I was in trouble. And thanks to Tracey and Hal for putting me up. And Kolby and Ted for giving Ricky and me some alone time together at the bunkhouse. Most of all, I wanted to say that

Ricky and I have something to share." She leaned over and kissed him and he kissed her back, so glad she wanted to tell everyone they were officially mated. She lifted his hand in hers. "We're mated."

Everyone cheered so loud, whistling, and calling out congratulations, Ricky thought the whole roof would collapse on them.

Ricky said, "This was meant to happen from the moment we were born in the same hospital, separated, rejoined each other, and separated again. It was like we had our own magic time machine that continued to reunite us until we finally knew we had to make this commitment. We'll be planning a wedding in the near future. Hang onto your steampunk duds. It'll be a steampunk wedding for sure."

Everyone cheered again and he couldn't be happier that they were back together again with a whole new family. When they left the podium, individuals came over to congratulate them, all the ladies wanting to help Mandy plan the wedding.

"A honeymoon?" Shannon, Chase's wife, asked.

"Uh, I think we'll stick to cougar territory for now," Mandy said. "At least until I know I have the shifting totally under control."

"Maybe we'll take a camping trip under the stars and near the waterfall beyond Hal and Tracey's property," Ricky said.

Then the conversations died down when someone new arrived at the community center. Edgar's brothers. Ricky wished he wasn't holding a steampunk rifle that was nothing more than a fun prop and was wearing his handgun instead.

The men didn't look like they were armed, at least.

Dan and Stryker went to speak to them, and they turned to see where Ricky and Mandy were and spoke to Dan and Stryker, then motioned to Ricky and his mate.

He didn't want her to come with him when he joined Dan and Stryker, but she stuck to him.

"We want to identify our brother's body. We don't want any trouble," the darker haired brother said.

"We want hear from them what really happened and take his body home," the other brother said.

Ricky guessed Dan had gotten ahold of them and told them the details of what had happened and that their brother was in the morgue. Ricky was past ready for this business with Edgar and his brothers to be over and done with. But he wished he could have left Mandy at the party while he dealt with this.

MANDY APPRECIATED that Ricky didn't want to trouble her with Edgar's brothers, but she needed to have resolution. She figured she'd have nightmares about being trapped in the trunk of the car, water filling it up, and nearly drowning her for some time over it.

When they arrived at the morgue, she didn't look at the body again, but she explained what had happened to her in detail. The brothers listened and then the one nodded.

"We tried to talk him out of looking for you. We told him you had chosen someone you knew before he'd even met you, but he wouldn't listen. We were afraid it would come to something like this. He didn't want you to be with anyone else, but we're glad you survived. Unless you need to hold his body for any other reason, we'd like to arrange to have him shipped home so we can bury him."

"He's all yours," Dan said. After they made arrangements, the brothers left, and the rest of them went back to the party.

Things had quieted down and Mandy was afraid that the

brothers' arrival had put a damper on the party, but then she and Ricky took to the dance floor to prove that they were ready to continue to party. This was one Halloween she would never forget, and she loved the cougars of Yuma Town for welcoming her into the family.

EPILOGUE

Seven months later, Ricky and Mandy had their steampunk wedding, and were moving into their new home near the creek. She couldn't have been any happier.

For now, they were packing for their camping trip near the Haverton's ranch for their honeymoon. A fancier honeymoon somewhere else would come later when she was sure her shifting wouldn't cause trouble.

She didn't think they'd make it to the car before Ricky was hauling her to bed again. Sure enough, he scooped her up and said, "Let's take a break before we head on out."

His idea of a break was having heart-thumping sex. That was all right by her. She was looking forward to camping with him too since they hadn't done that since they'd parted ways years earlier.

"Do you ever think of what could have been if I hadn't run into you that night on Friday, the thirteenth?" she asked, pulling off his shirt.

"I was meant to be on that road in the fog at that very same time," he said, kissing her. "I was meant to stop you in the only way that would have enough of an impact to really keep you with me."

She smiled and ran her hands through his hair. "Did I ever tell you I was sorry for running into you?"

He chuckled. "No, but you told me you loved me, and that's all that counts."

Then they were kissing and stripping, and she couldn't have been any happier than she was now.

THAT NIGHT, sitting beside the campfire near the waterfall near the Haverton's land and breaking open fortune cookies after having burgers over the fire, Ricky read his fortune out loud. "A person's character is his destiny."

Mandy opened hers and smiled. "What would be the odds that we'd have the same fortune?"

"No way. Let me see." Ricky read her fortune and laughed. "We're Libras—we are the balance in each other's life. We were meant to be."

They saw a falling star, but they didn't need to wish on it. All their dreams had already come true.

ACKNOWLEDGMENTS

Thanks to Donna Fournier and Darla Taylor for always being such great beta readers. I'll never forget the first time I asked Donna if she'd beta read for me, and she was thinking in terms of alpha and beta wolves and that didn't set right with her until I explained it just meant she'd read my story first and help to catch any of my mistakes. She could still be an alpha beta reader. Thanks, ladies, it means the world to me.

ABOUT THE AUTHOR

Author Bio

USA Today bestselling author Terry Spear has written over sixty paranormal and medieval Highland romances. In 2008, Heart of the Wolf was named a Publishers Weekly Best Book of the Year. She has received a PNR Top Pick, a Best Book of the Month nomination by Long and Short Reviews, numerous Night Owl Romance Top Picks, and 2 Paranormal Excellence Awards for Romantic Literature (Finalist & Honorable Mention). In 2016, Billionaire in Wolf's Clothing was an RT Book Reviews top pick. A retired officer of the U.S. Army Reserves, Terry also creates award-winning teddy bears that have found homes all over the world, helps out with her grandbaby, and she is raising two Havanese puppies. She lives in Spring, Texas.

She is on Wordpress at:
Terry Spear's Shifters
http://terryspear.wordpress.com/

And her Wilde & Woolley Bears, award-winning teddy bears, that have found homes all over the world: **www. celticbears.com**

www.terryspear.com

ALSO BY TERRY SPEAR

Heart of the Cougar Series:

Cougar's Mate, Book 1

Call of the Cougar, Book 2

Taming the Wild Cougar, Book 3

Covert Cougar Christmas (Novella)

Double Cougar Trouble, Book 4

Cougar Undercover, Book 5

Cougar Magic, Book 6

Cougar Halloween Mischief (Novella)

Falling for the Cougar, Book 7

Heart of the Bear Series

Loving the White Bear, Book 1

Claiming the White Bear, Book 2

The Highlanders Series: Winning the Highlander's Heart, The Accidental Highland Hero, Highland Rake, Taming the Wild Highlander, The Highlander, Her Highland Hero, The Viking's Highland Lass, His Wild Highland Lass (novella), Vexing the Highlander (novella), My Highlander

Other historical romances: Lady Caroline & the Egotistical Earl, A Ghost of a Chance at Love

Heart of the Wolf Series: Heart of the Wolf, Destiny of the Wolf, To Tempt the Wolf, Legend of the White Wolf, Seduced by the Wolf, Wolf Fever, Heart of the Highland Wolf, Dreaming of the Wolf, A SEAL in Wolf's Clothing, A Howl for a Highlander, A Highland Werewolf Wedding, A SEAL Wolf Christmas, Silence of the Wolf, Hero of a Highland Wolf, A Highland Wolf Christmas, A SEAL Wolf Hunting; A Silver Wolf Christmas, A SEAL Wolf in Too Deep, Alpha Wolf Need Not Apply, Billionaire in Wolf's Clothing, Between a Rock and a Hard Place, SEAL Wolf Undercover, Dreaming of a White Wolf Christmas, Flight of the White Wolf, All's Fair in Love and Wolf, A Billionaire Wolf for Christmas, SEAL Wolf Surrender (2019), Silver Town Wolf: Home for the Holidays (2019), Wolff Brothers: You Had Me at Wolf, Night of the Billionaire Wolf

SEAL Wolves: To Tempt the Wolf, A SEAL in Wolf's Clothing, A SEAL Wolf Christmas, A SEAL Wolf Hunting, A SEAL Wolf in Too Deep, SEAL Wolf Undercover, SEAL Wolf Surrender (2019)

Silver Bros Wolves: Destiny of the Wolf, Wolf Fever, Dreaming of the Wolf, Silence of the Wolf, A Silver Wolf Christmas, Alpha Wolf Need Not Apply, Between a Rock and a Hard Place, All's Fair in Love and Wolf, Silver Town Wolf: Home for the Holidays (2019)

Wolff Brothers of Silver Town

Billionaire Wolves: Billionaire in Wolf's Clothing, A Billionaire Wolf for Christmas

Highland Wolves: Heart of the Highland Wolf, A Howl for a Highlander, A Highland Werewolf Wedding, Hero of a Highland Wolf, A Highland Wolf Christmas

Heart of the Jaguar Series: Savage Hunger, Jaguar Fever, Jaguar Hunt, Jaguar Pride, A Very Jaguar Christmas, You Had Me at Jaguar (2019)

Novella: The Witch and the Jaguar (2018)

~

Romantic Suspense: Deadly Fortunes, In the Dead of the Night, Relative Danger, Bound by Danger

~

Vampire romances: Killing the Bloodlust, Deadly Liaisons, Huntress for Hire, Forbidden Love

Vampire Novellas: Vampiric Calling, The Siren's Lure, Seducing the Huntress

~

Other Romance: Exchanging Grooms, Marriage, Las Vegas Style

~

Science Fiction Romance: Galaxy Warrior

Teen/Young Adult/Fantasy Books

The World of Fae:

The Dark Fae, Book 1

The Deadly Fae, Book 2

The Winged Fae, Book 3

The Ancient Fae, Book 4

Dragon Fae, Book 5

Hawk Fae, Book 6

Phantom Fae, Book 7